The Gatekeeper

a novel by

C. Alease

Editing by Pentouch Editorial Services, Dallas, Texas
(www.pentouch.com)

To contact the author or to receive copies of this novel, please contact: c.alease@cadsmith.net

ISBN-10: 1449552641
ISBN-13/EAN-13: 9781449552640

Acknowledgements

This novel would not have been completed if it weren't for the blessings and guidance of my Father in Heaven, who gave me the story, the twist and the imagination to weave it into a work to be proud of. For that I am grateful beyond the written words He enabled me to put to paper. I am also eternally grateful to my family and dear friends for loving me unconditionally, and indulging my vivid imagination.

I want to acknowledge my wonderful friends and co-workers at the Trenton Housing Authority, Trenton, NJ (www.tha-nj.org), for their encouragement and prayers. I also wanted to sincerely thank Paula Hartman and Karla Pollack, of Association Business Solutions, Inc., Trenton, NJ, (www.absnj.com) for their encouragement and support.

For the Duchess, my babe, all my kids and my girls, and Rea

"Life is about creating yourself."

—George Bernard Shaw

Chapter One

Some of my best friends live inside my head. According to my therapist, a major trauma caused my mind to fragment into many personalities. So it appears that I am fragmented, though not completely split. The best way I can describe the condition—if such a condition exists—is that the people inside me are not jockeying for the top position in my mind. We all agree to disagree, and for the most part peacefully coexist. At different times, I have been convinced that one or more of these people took over and handled things for me while I stayed safe in the background. I didn't know there were others at first, and sometimes I don't believe what my therapist has concluded about my condition. But one thing is very clear: until I could put names and faces with these people, I really thought I was crazy.

It's not as though I really thought I was insane—just a bit touched, so to speak. But that's normal. The way I looked at it, at the very least everybody's a bit touched. That's what life does to folks. Sometimes it touched in places, and sometimes it smacked. Sometimes it kissed and caressed, and felt the way my favorite flowers smelled in spring. Sometimes it beat, bit, and bruised, and sometimes it even left a scar or twenty. That's just the way life was and for the most part, I thought I lived a pretty good one.

I wasn't any different from other winter babies born in New York City. My mother was just a kid herself, about twenty, by the time I came. Mom was stunning, beautiful by any standard. She was thin back then and only gained weight "after I had my children," she would say. From the pictures she'd kept of herself, she could have easily been a pinup girl or even a movie star.

According to my mother, she ran away from home in Philadelphia at fifteen, after my grandmother's husband tried to molest her and my grandmother chose him. In the Bronx, she moved in with my grandmother's brother, who was married with two young boys. While at a friend's apartment one evening, she met my father, fresh from the war in Korea. They got married after she got pregnant with my brother, Edward. When Edward was six weeks old, my mother went to her doctor for a routine checkup. She said the doctor and nurse laughed when they told her she was pregnant again. That made Edward ten months older than me.

It wasn't long before my mother learned my father liked poking his penis into her girlfriends, his girlfriends, or any females he happened upon. Her friends said they wouldn't have been surprised if he had children in Korea. He already had two children from another woman before my parents got together. Mom said she tried to stay with my father and make a home for us in New York, but that she was so young. "Naïve," she told me.

Even after she learned that her best friend and my father made a baby boy—around the same time she and my father conceived my brother and was pregnant with me—she still didn't leave him. She stayed with him until we moved in with my father's mother. That was around the time he strayed with the woman who eventually became his wife, a woman he stayed with until he died.

My mother moved us to Philadelphia when I was about four. The children in the neighborhood and most of the people we met told my mother they thought we were foreign, that we "talked proper," and that we looked like we came from another country. My mother liked those assessments. She took pride in making sure we were neat, clean, and well mannered all the time. If we didn't keep our room clean, my mother would go on the "warpath." That's what my Nana would call it. She'd say, "You better clean up that room, or your mother will go on the warpath with you children." Whenever we visited other people, she demanded we be polite and respectful, courteous and congenial. Mother corrected our speech to make sure we used the proper English all the time, "So you can be understood," she'd say. She didn't allow words like "ain't," and we knew better than to use slang—at least around her.

Although constantly told I was a pretty child, I never saw what others saw. I thought I was just ordinary, definitely not ugly, but not as pretty as people often remarked. People would say to my mother, "Your daughter is very beautiful," or "You have such a pretty little girl," or "Isn't she cute?" I only thought that girls with long hair deserved that kind of talk. My hair wasn't exceptionally long, although I sure wished it was, which is why I developed such a proclivity for hair extensions as an adult.

As a child, I often had nightmares, sometimes scaring me so much I would run through the dark into my Nana's bedroom and climb into bed with her. In one of the dreams, I would be standing by the window of my brother's and my bedroom. The sky was always just getting dark, with colors of deep purples, aqua, and pinks mixed in with the deep blues and grays. Then, like clockwork, I would hear a sound from far off, like a factory whistle, or air raid siren. Then, in the distance, I would see a small patch of black. The patch of black would grow as it moved toward me at the window, like a huge swarm of locusts, until it became distinguishable as black birds coming for me. Although in the dream there would be curtains on the window, by the time the birds got close enough to be distinguished, the curtains would disappear. I would try to move from the window but couldn't, and it always seemed the birds would get close enough to get me. Then I'd wake up. The birds always frightened me because they always seemed determined to get me, perhaps to take me somewhere I didn't want to go.

The one dream that always sent me running into Nana's bedroom was where a man draped in silhouette would come into my room, most times from behind the dresser with the mirror, but on occasion from behind the chest of drawers. He would slowly walk toward me, brandishing a large, shiny knife. The dream always ended swiftly; he never got close enough to me because I would always wake up as soon as I saw the knife and run out of my room. Then there was the dream I was running on Federal Street, looking behind me as if I was being chased, but no one was ever there. I always attributed that dream to the bad little boy who lived on the block who for some reason always threw bricks and chased me. Later I would learn he had a crush on me.

My growing pains were not unlike most children's. Nana called me a "maggot in hot ashes." It sounded bad, but it was actually a term of endearment Nana used whenever I fluttered about the house chatting up a storm. She would laugh and say to me, "Slow down, baby, you're just like a maggot in hot ashes, running a mile a minute." Most times, I was her "Chiddly-Diddly." Just to be close to my Nana, I would fight my brother for the chance to sit behind her legs on the couch while we watched TV together. Sometimes, after a particularly bad fight with my brother, she would warn me. "You need to mind that temper of yours. He's your brother. You are supposed to love him. Don't get so mad!"

When my mother moved us into Nana's house, Nana gave Mom the downstairs apartment, which had a living room, one bedroom, a kitchen, and bath. Depending on the way my mother arranged her furniture from time to time, getting to the kitchen or the bathroom meant walking through the living room and through the bedroom, or the bedroom through the living room. Nana put my brother and me in the bedroom upstairs from hers, in her apartment. We shared the room until he moved in with our father in New York when he was about thirteen.

I never thought of myself as especially bright. My brother was the smart one. He skipped an entire grade at school, jumping from fifth to seventh in one year. I always felt I was about average and had to struggle to keep my grades on par with his. In order to be rewarded for my grades, I had to maintain at least what he brought home, which were generally all *A*s. Until junior high, I managed to keep up most of the time, but became a bit preoccupied with breasts—or the lack of them, in my case. When my girlfriends from school were developing breasts and I was still flat, I thought I would never grow any and said as much to my mother one night when she was washing up in our tiny bathroom, getting ready to go out.

"Mommy," I cried, "I'm abnormal."

As she splashed water on her own voluptuous breasts, having gained considerable weight over the years, she raised one up, flapping it against her chest wall, and then the other. "Look at your mother! Don't worry. Believe me, you'll have plenty!"

I always thought my mother had a special predilection for the number fifteen, especially before I turned fifteen. She said I couldn't wear a garter belt or stockings until I reached fifteen, and I wasn't allowed to wear lipstick or eyeliner until I was fifteen. "No boy company until you are fifteen," she would say. My life wasn't supposed to begin until fifteen, I thought, and I was jealous of my friends because they were wearing stockings, full makeup, and having boys over. In fact, my friends were having sex before they were fifteen. Of course, that was out of the question for me, though. I didn't even want to think about sex and was proud to be a virgin until I was eighteen. Ironically, the first breast buds appeared on my flat chest—enough that the protrusion could be seen through an undershirt—when I turned fifteen. It's also when the eagle landed for me, so to speak; I got my period at fifteen. I met my first husband when I was fifteen. From that point on, I was convinced my mother was supernatural. She knew "all."

I always said that I attracted the wrong kind of men: fools, derelicts, transients, and babies. After just a few weeks with them, something would tell me each was no good, but then something else would keep me with them. I often thought that if only I had a father to raise me, perhaps I would have been able to make better choices in men. That's why I was so concerned about my youngest son, David. When I divorced Milton, he stayed out of David's life, and I felt extremely guilty about it. My son was gloomy, and it broke my heart to see him so sad. My other two children had my first husband, Gilbert, such that he was—in and out of jail, but more in than out, after I divorced him. I remember when I was about sixteen and was over his house waiting for him to show up. His mother spoke about him in a very not so motherly way.

"You see this chicken?" She held the chicken she was washing for dinner high in the air. "Gilbert is not even worth this chicken I'm cooking!"

By seventeen, I knew he was no good but thought I was in love. My mom and Nana always told me I thought I could change him, and that's why I stayed so long. Perhaps something inside thought so too. Milton, my second husband, wasn't much better, and I thought I loved him as well. At least I wised up before I stayed with him as long as I'd stayed with Gilbert.

So here I was—fifty-four years old, bubbly and cheerful but not happy, sad but not depressed, depressed but not suicidal, suicidal but not dead, and then bubbly all over again. Two failed marriages, the third one on and off the brink, a whole host of other losers, and three grown children later, I felt lost. I wondered about myself on and off all my life and never quite felt like I had it all together. Somehow, though, I always managed to keep up appearances. I always figured it was my job; that in order to make sure my family was happy, I let them think I was, too.

One day while on a lunch break with my friend Marissa from work, she began talking about being in therapy. She talked about "issues" from her past that, prior to therapy, had remained unresolved. "Nothing earth shattering," she said. "Just that I always felt somewhat invisible."

I was intrigued. She told me that the therapist helped her discover why she felt that way, and she felt rejuvenated as a result. I had noticed she was smiling more, and things didn't seem to stress her at work anymore.

I confided that I thought my youngest son might be having abandonment issues, because unlike my other two children from my first husband, he had no contact with his dad. I hoped that perhaps he would open up to someone more objective since I wasn't having any success getting him to talk about his anger issues.

I asked Marissa if her therapist was taking patients, and she handed me his card. "Oh, this therapist is the best! Much better than the ones I went to before him. His name is Dr. Wendell Townes. He attended a seminary and was ordained. He even prays with you during each session." With a review like that, I was positive he would be able to help my son, but I would still research him first. I discovered that this therapist was indeed a noted psychiatrist and psychotherapist. His many published papers were based on his research and counseling techniques. He had written a number of articles and had even published two textbooks on personality disorders. Satisfied that he was worth his salt, I called him and made an appointment for David.

Chapter Two

The therapist's office was a journey from where I worked, about a forty-five minute drive through winding highways and beautiful country scenery. When we pulled into the parking lot, a couple of deer were wandering toward the forest that faced the back of the building. Being a city girl, I was stunned by them, probably more than they were by me. After acknowledging the beautiful lilacs along the windows and picking a few for myself, my son and I walked into the office building and took seats in the waiting room.

Our appointment was for 4:00 p.m. "He's late!" I barked to my son. "I can't stand it when people are late! It's not professional. He'd better have a good damn reason."

My son looked at me and smiled. "Mom," he said, "It's only fifteen minutes. Why do you get so angry? Stop sweating the small stuff." He laughed, walked over to me, and kissed me on the cheek, knowing he could always calm me down that way.

The time had drifted to 4:50 before the therapist walked into the waiting room to greet us.

When he entered, my anger subsided. He was a heavyset, gentle-looking giant with a soft voice, friendly eyes, and a warm smile. He wore an old, worn light blue sweater over a blue checked shirt and a pair of jeans. *Very preppy,* I thought. I felt instantly at ease with him as he invited us into his office, and we engaged in a little small talk. I told him he'd been referred to me by one of my dearest friends and coworkers who I confided in generally and hoped he would be able to help my son. "And after you finish with David, I got some baggage that I want to get rid of myself," I said jokingly. I took a seat with my son on the couch while the therapist took a seat on a gently used wing chair across from us.

After filling out a few insurance papers, he began to ask my son a series of questions while I observed. He asked me only a few general questions and then requested I wait outside so he could speak with David alone.

I thought that perhaps he'd asked me to leave because I'd gotten angry when he asked me a question about Milton. When we divorced, Milton stayed away on his own, only resurfacing when David was fifteen. By then, I didn't even want David to be involved with him. When a mutual friend called one day offering to take David to a baseball game, he must have thought I was really gullible! This so-called friend was trying to set up a meeting with my son and Milton. It was all I could do not to reach into the telephone and pull out his throat!

It was difficult for me to wait outside without stewing like so many tomatoes in an Italian sauce pot. I always wondered if David blamed me for not having a relationship with his father, but Milton was a drug addict and womanizer. Undoubtedly, he wasn't the best example for my son to emulate, and I wasn't sorry for divorcing him. Still, misgivings about my son not having a father stressed me from time to time.

About forty minutes later, David and Dr. Townes emerged from his office. I searched my son's face for a glimpse into what he might have been feeling. He smiled when our eyes met and the therapist patted him on the back. "You have a great kid," he said. I already knew that and was hoping to hear something more akin to, "We have some work here to do." Instead, the therapist asked me to accompany him to his office and asked David to wait in the waiting room.

He asked me a few more questions about my life in general—nothing I found particularly threatening—and then asked me how I felt about David not having Milton around.

Quite unexpectedly, I flew into a rage that I suddenly felt I couldn't control. "He was a killer and a crack head! He was an abuser and slept around! I got Trichomonas from that cashier pig he worked with! I couldn't wait to get rid of that bastard!" I yelled so loudly I worried my son would hear what I was saying about his father. He was eighteen, and up until now I never talked about Milton's seamy side around him.

Dr. Townes seemed taken aback by my outburst, and so was I. Embarrassed and somewhat flushed, I sat up straight on the couch and apologized for shouting. He began taking notes. I wondered why he seemed so interested in me. "Aren't you supposed to be working on my son?" I asked.

The therapist stared at me, which made me feel all the more uneasy about him. Then with a swipe he removed his glasses from the tip of the bridge of his nose. "I'd like to see you again, if you don't mind." I agreed and made an appointment.

On the long drive home, I tried coaxing some information from my son—anything that would explain why the therapist was interested in me. "What did he ask you about me? Anything? What did you say to him?"

David just smiled and said, "I told him you were crazy. A good mom, but a little bit tapped." I took his remarks as the good-natured cracks I believed them to be and didn't ask any more questions about his visit.

David's visits were every two weeks, and for the next few months, I faithfully drove him to his appointments. Notwithstanding any halfhearted feelings about his progress or its lack thereof, David smiled more and more frequently around the house and seemed genuinely happier. Far be it for me to assume he wasn't being helped because he wouldn't discuss his therapy with me, and I certainly didn't want to pry into the inner workings of his sessions.

Typically, after about half an hour with my son, the therapist would summon me into his office to talk for the other half hour, mostly to ask why I hadn't made good on my own appointment with him yet. I politely declined to answer each time he asked, actually preferring to keep him out of my business. I had decided that therapy for me would be an enormous waste of time. After all, we were there for my son, not me. And certainly, as far as I was concerned, Dr. Wendell Townes' manner was a bit overbearing at the very least, and downright pushy at the most. I decided I didn't like him at all and would only tolerate him as long as he was helping my son, and that would be that. *So there*, I thought, as we left his office for the long drive home.

On David's next scheduled visit, I decided I would ask the questions. I was going to ask him about David's therapy. I was going to ask what he thought about my son's progress. *This will most assuredly keep the focus off me,* I thought.

The day we left for my son's scheduled visit was warm and muggy. The therapist's office was hot and steamy, even though the air conditioner was on full blast. I didn't envy my son when he went into the office first and was feeling quite a bit less interested in discussing his progress on such a hot day. *Perhaps it can wait until the office is a bit less muggy,* I thought, not at all in the mood to roast my skin on the outside or my insides from anger during the therapist's third degree.

When Dr. Townes finally summoned me, I immediately tried to talk my way out of visiting with him, but he was too adept at wheedling me into some sort of engagement whether I wanted to or not. Undaunted, it seemed, by my constant references to the sweltering heat in his office and the constant distraction I created by my incessant fanning with a magazine I took from the waiting room, he pressed me to make an appointment for myself.

Finally, I interrupted him and asked about my son's progress. "Doctor, all these months I have entertained you with funny anecdotes about me, my family, and friends. You have never used my son's other half hour of therapy on anyone but me. I never even asked questions about his progress. So, Doctor, just how the hell *is* he progressing anyway?" I was hoping that finally his spotlight on me would turn off.

Dr. Townes got up from his chair and walked over to his desk. He shuffled around some of the papers and other debris and found a dingy rag. Then he took off his glasses and wiped them with it. When he put his glasses back on, he walked over to the couch where I was sitting and sat down next to me. "There's nothing wrong with your son. It's *you* I need to see."

Chapter Three

Week One

My first solo visit with this wretched therapist and I was apprehensive to say the least, although something inside made me feel like I had reason to be there. Without a doubt, it would turn out to be an enormous waste of time. Or maybe I would actually feel rejuvenated after the experience, just like Marissa had suggested.

I sat in the sparse waiting room, looking around at the much of nothing there save for a few chairs and a magazine rack filled with old, torn travel and sports magazines. The therapist was late again—a fact which exasperated my insides, causing me to exercise every ounce of civility I could muster to keep from letting him have the full barrel of cuss words I had assembled just for him. Instead, I took a long, deep, and deliberate breath and followed him into his office, sat on the couch, and waited politely for him to prepare himself for my session.

After filling out my insurance papers, he placed them on his disheveled desk where I was sure they would get lost in the mess. He then sat in his chair and told me to relax and make myself comfortable. I was already as comfortable as I was going to allow myself to be under the circumstances and wasn't interested in following any of his suggestions. He tried to assure me everything was fine and that we were only going to chat. He asked me if I was a grandmother and I mentioned my many grandchildren. He asked if any were from my daughter, and I told him my grandchildren were my son's kids, as well as friends' children I had "adopted" over the years. We talked more about my extended family, something I enjoyed a great deal. Before I knew it, the clock on the therapist's wall read 5:00 and my session was over.

Not too bad, I thought. *The session wasn't too eventful, and not too threatening, either.*

The therapist sat back at his desk, shoved some of the papers away to reveal an appointment book, and asked if he could see me again the next week. I politely nodded a clear, but reluctant "Yes" and went on my way.

Week Two

The weather was brutal during the week, and the air conditioning at work had died. My meeting with the director of marketing, who knew just how to push all the wrong buttons, lasted two hours. I dubbed her the Albatross for her ability to dangle about my neck and swell my insides almost to boiling, a feeling worse than my hot flashes on a normal day. I was disgusted because she had stolen a project I'd mentioned I was planning to start a few weeks later. When I discovered during the meeting she'd stolen it and was taking full credit, I dug down deeply into my resentment and pulled out a stunning bouquet of fury, wrapped up neatly and perfectly, pretty and professional—which I then presented to her, the gift she deserved. I let her have it, *all* of it. Afterward, she needed to take the rest of the day off, and I was content—smug and content with the knowledge that I had, at least for that day, removed the Albatross from around my neck.

I certainly wasn't in any mood for my session. My first visit might have been uneventful, but I wasn't sure what the rest were going to bring. Besides, I was still eager to fight after my meeting with the Albatross. *He had better not make me angry today*, I thought.

When I arrived at the therapist's office, I sat in the car for a few minutes to calm down. There was really no point in taking out any anger on him; I'd already had my fill. After I had calmed down to a slow simmer, I sat in the waiting room. I watched the two children who were in there before me playing with some old toys the therapist kept for use when parents were in session.

Around 4:35, Dr. Townes emerged from his office with the parents who scooped up the kids, said their goodbyes, and left.

"They stole some of my time," I quipped. Dr. Townes ignored my obvious sarcasm and motioned for me to join him.

"Today," the therapist began, "I plan to take you to a place you will find safe and secure."

I asked, "Are we leaving the building?"

He said we wouldn't have to leave and repeated that it would be a place I would find safe and secure. He asked me to get comfortable and to relax. Still a bit confused, I obliged and took off my shoes, cuddled with a teddy bear he kept on the right side of the couch like a pillow, and made myself comfortable. He turned down the light in his office and asked me to close my eyes.

He began to speak in hushed tones. "Relax," he said. "Close your eyes and listen to the clicking sound of the clock on the wall."

I felt a bit silly and slightly embarrassed. Nevertheless, I closed my eyes and counted the clicking sounds of the clock, one click at a time.

He continued. "I want you to locate the beautiful garden. When you see the beautiful garden, I want you to start walking through it." He told me to look at the beautiful garden with the tree to the left of center and then to look ahead at the large Victorian house. As he instructed me to walk up the wooden steps to the porch of the house, he told me to notice the chairs on the porch. One chair was rocking back and forth, gently against the mild breeze. I walked up the worn, white wooden stairs that creaked beneath my feet and onto the equally weathered wooden porch. Then I stopped short of the large red double doors with the glass panes and lace curtains.

"Open the door and enter the foyer." I entered as my therapist described my surroundings. "There is a large round table in the center with a beautiful, thick oriental rug under it." I saw the table with a large vase filled with flowers that smelled like the perfume I wore that day, and the rug was thick and cushy. He said I could change anything about the house that I wanted because it was my house.

I still felt completely aware of my surroundings outside of the house and inside of the therapist's office. It was a strange sort of feeling. My eyelids were closed and fluttered uncontrollably. Although I felt like I could open them at any time, when I tried I couldn't. I clutched the teddy bear close to my chest and continued to watch the panoramic visions in my head.

"There are two large doors that open into another room with large windows that overlook the beautiful garden outside," he said. I ran into the room and headed directly to one of the large bow windows.

"There is a fireplace with a fire burning. Remember, this is your room. You can change your room any way you want it to look. This is your Safe Room," he said. "I want you to be comfortable here."

I looked around the room and noticed there were no curtains on the large bow windows on either side of the fireplace, so I added pretty green and white flowered and striped drapes on the windows and placed a large round table in the center of the room. I added pictures of flowers.

Then the therapist asked, "Who is in the room with you?"

"Just me."

He asked, "What are you wearing?"

"I have on my pretty dress that my mommy bought me, with a white pinafore on it, and my hair is in ponytails. I have on white socks with ruffles and black patent Mary Janes."

He asked, "What are you doing?"

I was looking out the large bow window on the right side of the fireplace I had just adorned, staring at the big tree that was slightly to the left of center outside. It was breezy, and the sun was shining on my face. My head rested in my hands, which were facing the sill, my head tilted slightly. Somewhat confused, but intrigued that I was able to make things appear and disappear at will, I danced in circles, twirling around, the wide parts of my dress raising and spinning like an enthusiastic dance partner. I jumped on the big cushy couch my therapist said was in the room, but I turned it into one even more fluffy and comfy.

When I flopped down on the cushions, my therapist asked me to join myself in the room.

What an absolutely strange request, I thought. I looked around the room. Certainly I was already in the room, but when asked I'd described some little kid. "But how can I do that?"

"Just bring yourself into the room as you are right now, with the clothes you are wearing right now."

This was absurd. Wasn't I was already there? I didn't see myself, only the little girl, so how was I going to bring myself into the room, especially if I felt I was already there?

Perhaps if I just concentrate hard on what I have on today... I thought. *Then I will just see myself in the room, and there I'll be.* I concentrated on myself as I was dressed when I arrived in the therapist's office and brought myself into the room, which turned out to be easier than I'd thought. I was in the room with the little girl and stood there staring at her. She stared back.

Dr. Townes began the formal introductions. "Meet Little Me. This is your little self, the you that you really are."

Chapter Four

Hmmm, *Little Me,* I thought. We stared at each other, silently sizing each other up, but in a good way, all the while feeling extremely awkward about being face to face with myself and not quite knowing what to do about it. She was so cute though, with such wide, bright eyes, full of delight in her surroundings, and smiling at me, smiling with the big fish mouth my dad said I had. I shrugged off the therapist's explanation of her as the "me that I really was." After all, she was a child and I was an adult. Perhaps he was going to feed me that inner child bullshit that shrinks say we all have. Little Me stretched out her tiny arm, hand opened, and took it into my hand. I followed her to the big cushy couch and we sat together. She let go of my hand when she jumped onto the couch, her tiny cola bottle legs swinging back and forth because they were too little to reach the bottom of the couch.

For a while, there was silence as I looked around the room. We were two people in that room, a prospect which both frightened and beguiled me. We looked at each other, smiled, and then looked away, pretending to be more interested in the room's surroundings than each other, every now and then sneaking side-eyed looks and smiling politely.

Suddenly, we were startled by the voice of Dr. Townes asking, "What are you doing now?"

"We are looking at each other and smiling. I think she likes me," I said.

Then he asked, "Little Me, who is the one who wants to die?"

Shocked by Dr. Townes' question and incredulous about the direction I thought he was taking, I jumped up from the sofa, stared into the air in the Safe Room, and shouted, "Nobody!" I began to feel extremely agitated by his suggestion that I was suicidal. Why was he bringing that up?

His tone became much gentler and a great deal less condemning. I imagine it was because he could tell how angry I was getting. "Little Me, bring in the one who wants to die. It's all right. You are in your Safe Room and she will be safe as well."

Little Me slid her tiny body off the couch and stared around the room, peering around furniture as though someone were there but out of view. Then suddenly, a smoky gray haze began to enter the room, rising into the air and erupting into a fiery flame; not the kind of flame that burns but a flame of light, forceful and mighty.

"What do you see?" he asked.

Startled, I said, "Smoke, fire, bright light. Someone is here. I don't think it's the one who wants to die. I can't really make out the form because it is too smoky and too bright to see through."

A form was growing through the haze. "I think it's a man." I looked harder and didn't see a man's form. "No, I don't see a man, it looks like a woman. Yes, it is a woman," I concluded.

The therapist wanted to know more about the woman who arrived through the fiery inferno. "What does she look like?" he asked.

I walked around the smartly dressed woman and looked her over. She had on a dark, tailored suit with a crisp white button-down oxford shirt. Her hair was very short and curly, wet looking, and immaculately coifed.

"It's the Masculine One," Little Me said.

Dr. Townes began to speak to the Masculine One. "Who are you?"

"I am the only one who gives a damn about our well being, the only one who actually protects us. Even when the others try to overrule me, I will keep trying to protect us."

"Others? Overruling?" I asked, confused by her preposterous assertion that there were others. *What's going on?* I thought nervously.

The Masculine One ignored my question and continued. "Just like now. I didn't ask to come here, and I tried to tell everybody that this was a stupid-assed idea, coming here to talk to you when we were just fine the way we were. I make my presence felt when I need to, and I don't really give two shits about what you think."

What others? I thought, even more anxious over the prospect that I was missing something I should know about. The Masculine One appeared to be very angry and shouted as though she knew other people were listening.

"The others can kiss my ass right now, because they all overruled me on this one, but I know this shit is a waste of time. I am not a crybaby. I am not interested in rehashing our life. I never liked reading stories where the protagonist whines incessantly about how bad life was before the great uplifting. Human existence is filled with stories of triumph and tragedy, hope and despair. Our life is no different from millions of others, worse than millions of others, and not as bad as millions of others."

This woman was hell, fire, and brimstone, full of rage. She frightened me. I sat back on the couch and drew Little Me close while the Masculine One paced back and forth along the fireplace between the two large bow windows.

"I am not purging today, and no damn shrink can make me! I don't feel the need to regurgitate my life so some fucking shrink can write a book on my dime to get an interview and book push from the big O woman. I don't need redemption! I am not making excuses for our life, and I am not blaming anyone, either. Our guilt, our fear, our overindulgence, our shame; these things prepared us for the triumph we enjoy now. And know that I can kick your ass in a heartbeat if you tread on me." A cloud of red and yellow smoke rose from her head like an exclamation point to her rant.

I stared at the woman in the dark suit with the white cotton oxford shirt, starched collar and cuffs. She looked just the way I liked to look sometimes. She wore lovely and tasteful gold jewelry on her ears, neck, and wrist, just the way I like to wear my jewelry, not gaudy or over the top. I bet she must have been the woman my daughter said I was when I worked for the law firm. The "Corporate Dyke" is what my daughter called me; not because she thought I was gay but because of the way I dressed. Nevertheless, when I stared at her, like Little Me, I felt she was a part of me, and now we were three.

"I am placing four angels around the four corners of your room, and they will protect you now. I want you to see that Jesus has entered the room." Dr. Townes then began a prayer. "Suffer the little children… come unto me …" Jesus stood at the fireplace and stretched out His arms. He brought Little Me into His arms and held her tightly to Him. Dr. Townes asked the Masculine One to go to Jesus. She protested but obliged, disappearing into Him. Then Little Me disappeared into Him. Finally, Jesus disappeared into me, as I was that day, dressed as I was dressed that day.

"As you walk out of your Safe Room and into the foyer, you notice the large table with the beautiful flowers. You walk to the large red double doors and open them wide to reveal a bright, beautiful sun shining down on you. As you walk down the stairs, you notice the big tree, to your right, now. You are in my office again, and you are happy."

The therapist turned up the light in the office, and I was back, remembering clearly where I had been, but feeling oddly at ease. He diagnosed me and said I had some long name for crazy called *DDNOS*. According to him, I met one of the people who have been protecting Little Me. What's more, there were probably others, and Little Me is supposedly brilliant to have created these others living in my head. After only a couple of visits, he decided I had some kind of personality disorder. In complete disbelief, but intrigued nonetheless, I made another appointment for the next week.

Week Three

I had a difficult time trying to absorb the prospect of having two other people living within my mind; people who were unique but not the typical kind one would associate with the movies I'd seen about conditions like this. The only references close to what he was talking about I had seen in movies, and I certainly didn't consider myself the same as Sybil or Eve. *They were nuts,* I thought. In fact, when I Googled the word fragmented, I got well over a million hits related mostly to dissociation, and dissociation had everything to do with multiple personality disorders where the person was unaware of the others. I pondered the possibility that I might be fragmented, or more importantly, dissociated. Weren't both the Masculine One and Little Me unknown to me before I started therapy? I wasn't even aware of Little Me or the Masculine One before I went into the Safe Room.

That's it; I'm a loon, maybe even schizophrenic! But I can't be schizophrenic, because schizos hear voices in their heads. I laughed nervously to myself. *If this therapist says I'm fragmented, then I'll take this trip he's trying to take me on. Besides, what kind of trauma did I suffer in the first place to fragment myself into the me that I am most of the time, and that fireball I met the week before? What's more, I'm grown. Where is this Little Me coming from, and why does my therapist say she is the best part?*

I visited my therapist again at 4:40 p.m. on our third scheduled Wednesday afternoon, dressed in a very smart navy Jones New York pants suit, crisp cotton Liz Claiborne oxford shirt, and navy patent sling-back flats from Talbot's Online I'd bought with the gift certificate from my daughter last Christmas.

After a short wait, my therapist appeared with his fatherly smile and invited me into his office. "That Little You," he began, "is the best part of you. I really like her. She is really smart. When I speak to you, I want her to answer."

I was perplexed. *How the heck do I summon Little Me outside of the Safe Room?* I thought. Frankly, I didn't really believe this Little Me existed. This therapist was assuming far too much of me and what I could do. After all, this was all very new to me.

Dr. Townes looked me up and down, but not the way men usually looked, and said, "You look very nice today." He continued, "You look like the way you described that masculine lady in the Safe Room."

I looked at myself and inspected what I was wearing. He was correct. Evidently, I dressed like the Masculine One would dress, and she was me all day. I thought I had chosen that suit because I knew I was going to have to deal with my Albatross at work. Navy blue and white makes me feel intelligent and confident. I knew I would have to be confident enough to stand up to that bitch today. Strange though—only after the therapist mentioned how I looked did the prospect of the Masculine One influencing the way I dressed even occur to me. As a matter of fact, I didn't believe she existed.

Dr. Townes went on to say he would be able to tell when he was dealing with someone other than me. That was really spooky. *Could he be psychic?* I thought facetiously.

I began our conversation talking about my day at work, dealing with the Albatross. Dr. Townes laughed and his eyes grew wide as he asked just who the Albatross was. I explained she was someone I worked with, the name given to her because she felt like an albatross around my neck. "A real bitch!" I exclaimed. "I can handle her though!" Shocked and embarrassed by my tone and use of profanity, I covered my mouth with my hand. Lately, I had been cursing and sputtering more and more, especially at work and even at home, and was trying to curb some of the language, mainly because of my impressionable grandchildren.

He excused me and asked, "What does your Little Me think of her?"

I shrugged and put my head down. Suddenly, a tremendous ache in my skull overtook me. The pain engulfed me, and I couldn't think. My head fell to my breasts and felt like it would fall completely off. Then I slowly raised my head and exhaled a deep sigh. I knew my mouth was moving, but it wasn't me talking. It was Little Me. I felt like I had been pushed back somewhere, and that she had stepped in front of my head. I felt different—strange to say the least.

"I don't like her. She makes me angry because she tries to make me feel stupid. I always think I have to prove to her I know what I am doing." Then as quickly as my head began to hurt, the pain subsided. I felt drawn quickly back to the front of my head and suspected immediately that it was because Little Me had gone back to wherever she was. She was real.

Townes changed the subject, dismissing the Albatross as someone with issues. I was grateful to move on. He said there were probably more people I would meet in my Safe Room and that he wanted to take me there as he had the week before. He would not be sure how many there were until we met them all. I was afraid of what to expect but at the same time was intrigued about the possibility of meeting more of myself. I was always drawn to subjects about the mind and fascinated with its inner workings. Indeed, if I was to believe the therapist at all at this point, I would have to keep the Safe Room doors unlocked for whoever might enter, with my mind's door at least cracked.

Satisfied he could begin, Townes dimmed the lights. I made myself comfortable on the couch, plumping a new pillow under my head and clutching the teddy bear.

"Concentrate on the sound of the clock on the wall," he said.

I was back in the front yard of the large Victorian house with the big, red double doors. *There's the tree!* I thought. I was running through the grass toward the house because I couldn't wait to get back to the room I had made for myself.

"As you open the doors to the house, you see the table with the vase of flowers, and you walk around the table ..." The therapist didn't know I had already pushed through the front doors and was looking with great pride at the newly painted French doors I'd made. After I made my way through the French doors, I threw my arms wide apart like airplane wings and whirled around my room, barely missing the big round table in the middle of the floor.

"Where are you?" he asked. I told him I was in my room playing. "Who are you?" he asked.

"I'm me," I replied.

"What are you wearing?"

"Jeans, some sneakers, and a top." I pointed to each piece that I described as I spoke to him. He asked how I was wearing my hair, and I replied, "Ponytails." I couldn't understand why Little Me was talking, and yet the words were coming from my mouth.

Then he said, "I would like you to bring the you that you are today, and the way you are dressed today, into the room with Little Me."

I supposed it was necessary to separate us from each other in the Safe Room, although I was still confused about it all. Still, it was easier for me to join Little Me in the Safe Room. I just thought about it, and there I was again, looking at Little Me. She came over to me and gave me a big hug about the waist, since she could only reach that far. "She's glad to see me!" I gushed.

He instructed the two of us to sit on the couch. Then he began to speak slowly and more softly than he usually did. "There's someone else in there with you."

I was watching Little Me jumping from cushion to cushion on the couch in the way I used to play hopscotch as a child. Neither of us was paying much attention to the therapist.

His voice grew a bit louder. "I want you to invite this person into the room with you."

I got up from the couch to see where the person was, but Little Me was already pointing to the French door that was open on the right side. Little Me screamed with delight as she opened the other side of the French door. "It's Big Fat! It's Big Fat!"

My God! I thought. *Big Fat?* Suddenly, this woman, this huge woman, so fat that her stomach swayed from side to side and dragged the floor as she walked, slowly meandered into the room and sat on the couch, breaking one of the legs. Her raucously loud laughter only intensified when she caught and held Little Me, who jumped into her pillow soft lap and seemed to disappear between the billowy layers.

Dr. Townes was sitting quietly; I imagined him taking copious notes. I sat on the couch, observing Big Fat.

Then he said, "I want Little Me to invite the Masculine One into the room."

Before either of us could respond, in a flash of fire, smoke, and fog, the Masculine One sauntered into the room, again immaculately dressed. She took a seat next to Big Fat on the couch. Dr. Townes asked Big Fat to introduce herself to us.

"Well, my little sweetie here knows who I am. I'm the one who loves food. I love food because it makes me feel good. I use it on the others of us, and sometimes I can get everybody on board for a good eat.

"I can cook better than most people. Our family loves the two times during the year when I really put it on thick. I'm up to twenty sweet potato *pas* on Thanksgiving and Christmas, because everybody wants my *pa*. Yeah, they don't even call it pie anymore; it's '*pa*.' Mom, they say, 'you make sure you get all the stuff for the *pas*.' Everybody gets at least one whole one now.

"I love truffles, especially the white chocolate ones! Those are my favorite. Most times I can get my way and get her to buy at least one bag when we are all out shopping. But when they are all watching her weight, I seem to get the raw end of the pork chop." Big Fat pulled out a laugh so loud and strong from the pit of her belly that her stomach and arm rolls quaked and quivered almost as violently as a powerful earthquake. Little Me grabbed the folds of soft billowy fat around Big Fat's waist and held on as she shook from side to side. As the quaking subsided, she soon disappeared back within Big Fat's massive, cushiony soft arms.

"I know Little Me likes candy and goodies, but she was never able to have much of it, so if I get a little selfish sometimes and give her all we want, it's because I love her, and far be it for me to deprive her, with all she's been through."

I was astounded. Big Fat was huge, massive. Was she part of me, too? I was a woman of substance so to speak, but I never thought that I had someone like that inside me. As far as I was concerned, she could stay inside and never come out unless we were in the Safe Room.

"Where is the one who wants to die?" Townes asked as he did the week before. Little Me shouted, "I know who she is. She's here, but she says she's too tired to come into the room. Sick and Tired is just outside."

The Masculine One appeared annoyed with the person Little Me spoke about and got up from the couch where she had been sitting quietly. She walked to the French doors, flung them open and brought in a disheveled young woman in her early twenties, wearing a dingy white T-shirt and a pair of dull black stretch pants with elastic around the waist. Her hair was uncombed and the frown on her lips only brought more attention to the dried tears on her ashy face. The Masculine One hurled her onto the opposite side of the couch where she landed with a thud. Stunned by the appearance of these individuals as a group, and especially the one called Sick and Tired, I stared at her as she rolled herself into a fetal position on the couch, and I informed the therapist she had arrived.

"Welcome to your Safe Room, Sick and Tired," the therapist began. "Can you let us know why you want to die?" Sick and Tired crouched into the corner of the couch all the way to the arm of it, so that she could rest her head in her hand. "Who are you and why do you wish to die?"

"I wouldn't say I want to die, though I do want to die sometimes. No. I don't want to die, but I do generally think it would be better if I was dead. I think I want to die, well, at least most of the time. This is my quandary of life, my quagmire, with muck so thick that I am drowning. I can't breathe, I'm gasping for air, but there's nothing but smoke making me choke. It's so dark, I can't see. I'm so tired. I just want to rest. I can't take it anymore."

There she sat in fetal position, such a miserable wretch of a woman, crouched in the corner of the couch. "Life for me ..." she began, "it ain't been no crystal stair, and there's no out for me other than the one that would make me leave the ones I love permanently. I would shoot myself but I am afraid of guns. I could take a bunch of pills, but I might just survive as a vegetable. Somehow, hurling myself off a bridge or a tall building doesn't appeal to me, either. We won't even talk about the mess stabbing myself might make. Good thing I am a coward, though. It's just a good thing that I am afraid that the others would probably kill me before they let me kill myself. That is the main problem of all the problems with my situation. If I end myself, it's not just me anymore. I am ending us."

I got up to get a better look at this Sick and Tired. Was she inside me, too? Without a doubt, I know I had been sick and tired before, but she was pathetic. Sick and Tired raised her head slightly and then slumped back into the couch.

"Langston Hughes and I are kindred spirits. No crystal stair spoke directly about me, you know. Sometimes all I think about is how my children will remember me after I'm dead. I think they would say, 'Mom could really make the best sweet potato pies!' But then, they'd be talking about Big Fat. They might say, 'Mommy always jumped to conclusions!' but they'd be talking about that fireball over there. Maybe they would say, 'Mom could talk! She would give a speech on just about anything!' Even then, they wouldn't be talking about me, they'd be talking about The Chatterbox. Living is a bitch and I know it. I could maybe be happy, but I'm too damn sick and tired most of the time to care about how to get there."

The Masculine One was incensed, pointing directly at Sick and Tired. "You see? She is one of the reasons why I spend most of the time trying to protect us. I have to protect us from her. She has tried, you know, to kill us. Well, not exactly, not yet, but she certainly called Suicide Prevention a few times, talking for hours and hours about how miserable we are." Big Fat recalled, "I remember the time when Sick and Tired called the Suicide Prevention people, talking about how she didn't want to kill herself for what seemed like hours. All the while, the Suicide Prevention people were on their way to our apartment! They were knocking on the door while she was on the phone with them!"

I was flabbergasted by the commotion brewing in the room by these three other distinct people and Little Me, all of whom the therapist purported to be parts of me. Until that moment, I thought calling Suicide Prevention was part of a crazy dream I had a long time ago. It seemed so real, but I thought it was all just a dream. I'd been in my mid-twenties; my first son, Michael was potty training and running around the house without his diaper. My daughter, Danielle was playing by herself on a blanket I'd placed on the living room floor for her. She could sit up by herself, grabbing at the assortment of toys I placed nearest to her. They were gleefully unaware that I was in the kitchen with the phone dialing Suicide Prevention. I really didn't want to kill myself and didn't know why I called them, although here I was, talking with them about how much I loved my children, and how much I didn't want to die, when suddenly there was a knock on my apartment door. Still talking to the person on the other end of the phone, I walked to the door and opened it to discover representatives from Suicide Prevention's outreach team at my door. I let them in, a little embarrassed and very surprised because I still had them on the phone. The thought that it really happened was unnerving. "Did that really happen?" I asked the others in the room. They all nodded their heads affirmatively.

The clock on the wall above the fireplace chimed at 2:00 p.m., and at the same time, the therapist advised that four of the angels were standing in the four corners of the room. Jesus appeared, and he began the prayer that he'd recited the week before. One by one, each rose from the couch and disappeared into Jesus. Big Fat was first, slowly, because of her vast dimensions, then the Masculine One, a great deal more annoyed now than in the previous week, and full of fire. Next, Sick and Tired walked slowly to Jesus with a tear in her eye and a deep sense of foreboding. Jesus took her into His arms, and she disappeared into Him. Then it was time for Little Me, who had left Big Fat's soft arms and was already in Jesus' arms. She disappeared into Him. Finally, Jesus walked over to the fireplace where I was standing and disappeared into me.

I followed Dr. Townes' instructions as he guided me from the room. "You see the large tree that is to your right; you are back in my office, and you are happy." He wanted me to talk with him about my childhood for our next scheduled visit. He felt that he would need to see me every week for the unforeseeable future.

As I contemplated the session driving the long drive home, I realized I'd probably been with Sick and Tired for a great deal of my life. But when did Big Fat join us? And for God's sake, I hoped the Masculine One was all bark and no bite. I definitely needed to know more.

Without warning, my hands grasped the steering wheel, and I found myself signaling to move from the left lane to the right, and then to the shoulder of the road. Suddenly there was a rush of voices in my head, which frightened me. I parked the car and sat motionless. There was an argument in my mind, and I wasn't in control.

"SHUT THE HELL UP!" one of the voices yelled.

"I've got to get home," another said. "I'll get us home," said another.

I finally recognized one voice as belonging to the Masculine One. My hands took the wheel, and the car pulled out into traffic and headed home. The voices had quieted down to whispers.

"I'm not going to be overruled tonight! We've got to get home," said the Masculine One.

Chapter Five

Week Four

I worked out a schedule with my boss so I could make my weekly Tuesday at 4:30 sessions on time. As I left my boss' office and tiptoed past Marissa's, I was startled when I noticed her already waiting at my door. I had been trying to avoid Marissa for the past three weeks, and she'd been trying to get me alone. I suspected that by now our therapist had to have told her I was also a patient and thought for sure he was running his mouth about me.

"So, what do you think of the good doctor?" she asked, blocking my way into my office.

"I don't like him," I said, prying her hands from the molding on either side of the door. "He's pushy, and he thinks he knows it all." I managed to loosen her grip long enough to get past her. "I don't have time to talk about him or my therapy."

I grabbed my pocketbook and rushed past her, pushing her a bit, but not so much as to knock her down. "I have to go for a session right now," I said, acknowledging her wide-eyed glare and distinct, budding obsession with my therapy visits.

Driving along the long, winding road to the therapist's office while the season was changing to Fall was beautiful to watch but not very easy to navigate in the dark, and it was getting dark a great deal earlier now. I wasn't particular about driving but didn't like driving in the dark.

I pulled into the parking lot and suddenly felt like turning around and making a run for it. *Oh, it's just Sick and Tired,* I thought.

"Just stop it. Everything will be fine," I said as I exited the car. I laughed aloud at the thought of recognizing one of my selves trying to surface, and then I looked around, only to discover the driver in the car next to mine was staring at me wildly. I quickly drew a sly grin and obnoxious stare and retorted, "And who doesn't talk to oneself from time to time?"

Townes was late, as usual. He must have had a trying time with the client before me. I waited patiently for about fifteen minutes before he came out, looking more haggard than usual. By the time he got to me, he almost always looked worn, but today he looked like he was canceling my session. Instead, he smiled and motioned for me to join him in his office. When I entered, he was already sitting in his tall wing back chair, which was haggard like him.

He wiped a small amount of sweat from his wrinkled brow. His eyes reached above the lenses of his glasses, and he looked over at me. "How was your day?"

"Evidently not as bad as yours; you were late." I apologized for the remark and blamed the Masculine One for it.

I was ambivalent about recognizing Sick and Tired for the first time out of the Safe Room. I was still intrigued, but uneasy about her existence.

"I had a moment where I actually recognized Sick and Tired in the parking lot. I thought I wanted to leave but realized it was Sick and Tired rising to the top. I could feel it!" I told the therapist. He nodded and then explained that as time went on, and I met everyone, I would be more able to determine which one was in the forefront.

Before we started our session, I asked him if I had lost time or repressed memories. "Doctor, how is it I didn't know Sick and Tired had called Suicide Prevention? Why did I think it was a dream?"

"You were there, but you were most likely pushed to the background while Sick and Tired was in charge." He put his tablet and pen down on the end table near his chair. "Let me explain what is going on with you." He demonstrated with his hand. He stretched his fingers wide apart on his left hand and said, "Each of these fingers is a part of Little Me. Little Me created them. Just like this hand, the fingers are still attached, just spread apart. There hasn't been a complete split, and that's a good thing. If Little Me had split entirely because of severe trauma, each of these fingers would try to take control of the hand at the expense of the others. Little Me is the one keeping you all together and allowing you to meet each other. Right now, although your parts are all still connected like the fingers on my hand, the fingers only have their particular purpose, nothing more."

He opened his hand again and spread his fingers wide apart, wiggling his thumb. "Your Little Me is right here. She keeps the hand together. She just needs to mature and grow properly." He then drew his fingers close together until they touched each other, then he clenched his hand into a fist. "When Little Me is healed through therapy, then all of these fingers will know what to do because they will be a complete hand, fully functional."

He leaned in closer to me. "One of the most important things I want you to do is to begin thinking of yourself as a survivor, because I believe that dissociation is a superb defense mechanism, a life saver. Think of your condition as a life saving response to your trauma and that you are a true survivor."

I nodded once, and then two more times, sighed and said "Oh, Okay," as though I completely understood his explanation, even though I really didn't. I couldn't wrap my head around the notion that I was even a victim, let alone a survivor.

Today was the day to discuss my childhood. *Where will I begin?* I thought. Should I start with the time we first moved to Philadelphia, or jump directly into when I was in school? Seeing as how there were these others to draw from, I pondered whether one of them would tell the story instead. How deliciously confusing it all was at this point; fascinating indeed, inasmuch as while I couldn't control *who* would come out to talk, when they did I was fully aware that the voices came from my mouth, from me. I felt giddy today and felt like nothing could rile me. I decided that whoever would chime in would certainly do so when the spirit moved, since my past was also theirs. Besides, it seemed they would probably know more than I did.

When it seemed no one was interested in starting, I began from where I remembered and where I thought the therapist would be most interested. "I was a precocious child, you know, smart as a whip," I said. "When I was five, I led a group of over one hundred kids in an athletic exercise during the Penn Relays. I used to write plays in school and my teacher would put on the productions for assembly. I—"

Dr. Townes interrupted me. "How do you feel about your mother?"

A voice crept into my head and blurted out of my mouth, "What the hell kind of question is that? We're supposed to talk about *me*. I don't want to talk about my mother. Why do I have to talk about my mother?" I covered my mouth. That embarrassed me, so I apologized again. All at once, voices in my head began to speak, loudly, some screaming to be heard. Some came out of my mouth faster than I could identify the voices. There was the Masculine One arguing about my mother; she definitely did not want to talk about her. Sick and Tired groaned and mumbled, but her voice didn't come out of my mouth. Big Fat complained about hunger. There were others in my head too, yelling and arguing and I could not identify them all. *My God!* I thought. *You've got to be kidding me!*

I sat up abruptly when a force stronger than I could control forced me to lean in closer to the therapist and point my finger at him. "My mother used to beat me!" I exclaimed. I was being controlled by something. I didn't want to tell him that. I covered my mouth again. Then my mouth abruptly filled up with words, so many that it felt like the floodgates containing a raging river, swelled from the sheer weight of water behind them, were ready to burst open. Then the gates exploded and the river poured out. I couldn't stop myself because I was no longer myself, and I could only listen and hope that the flood would crest and subside.

"My Nana raised me." This voice was raised and angry. "My mother used to beat me and my brother if our room wasn't clean. We got beat for some of the most outrageous things! Sometimes I was so scared coming home from school because I didn't know if she would be on the warpath. One day, my mother was washing a hat for me. It was one of those artificial fur hats with two ribbon ties and fur balls on the end of the ties. It looked like a brown and white muff, but for my head. She was washing it out, but I didn't know it. I was afraid because if I couldn't find something, my mother would beat me for losing it. She asked me for the hat and of course, I panicked. My Nana knew I was terrified and tried to help me find it, but we didn't know where it could be. I cried and fell on my knees praying to God to help me find my hat, so I wouldn't get a beating. Exhausted, cried out and terrified of what I was sure would happen next, I dragged myself into the bathroom to tell my mother that I couldn't find the hat only to see her washing it in the tub and laughing. 'See, you didn't even know where it was,' she said."

Dr. Townes stared at me above his glasses. I was convinced he didn't know who was talking, because I certainly didn't. "How did that make you feel when you realized your mother had the hat the whole time?"

"How could I possibly feel? I was relieved," said the voice.

Yet another voice I couldn't identify chimed in, moving in front of the one who was there before, pushing me further back. "One night, when I was about six, I decided I wanted to try a cigarette. So I took an old dried, bent cigarette butt—nothing really resembling tobacco still on it—and tried to sneak it and a pack of matches up to my room. Mom and Nana were in the living room and saw me walking toward the steps. I overheard my mom whisper to my Nana, 'She's up to something; I am going to see what she's doing.' Mom called to me to come down the stairs. 'Right now, and bring what you have in your hand.' She knew something wasn't right. 'I said, come back down here and bring what you have in your hand!' I'd made it to the top of the steps, had reached the hallway where there were bags filled with clothes. I grabbed an old sock and went back down to present it to my mom.

"When I showed her the sock, she looked at me and laughed like she'd just heard a really funny joke. She looked at Nana and then back at me with a grin, and then back at Nana. I stood there with the sock in my hand, waiting, waiting, and then she said, 'You did not go upstairs with this sock in your hand. Go back upstairs and bring down what you had.' I turned around and slowly walked up the steps, one step, two steps, until I was at the top staring at the cigarette butt and matches on the floor at the top step. I bent to pick them up, and turned to take the longest walk down those steps that I could. I knew I was in trouble, big trouble.

"I walked into the living room with my head down, terrified to face my mother. I stretched out my hand to reveal the cigarette butt and the matches. I raised my head to look at Nana for help, but she was staring at my mother with a peculiar look on her face. I couldn't tell if they were angry. Their eyes were wide and both their mouths had flung open and seemed to be smiling, just slightly. Then they began to laugh, loud and hard. They thought it was funny! I started laughing, too. It was all just good fun! I'd thought. Then my mom started spelling. They always spelled when they didn't want me to know what was being said. Mom said, 'I am going to give her a good b-e-a-t-i-n-g.' At first, I couldn't make out what she was saying because they were laughing between the words. Then I caught the letters when she repeated, 'B-e-a-t-i-n-g.' I cried, 'No, no, Mommy, pleeese don't give me a b-e-a-t-i-n-g!'

"I don't know exactly what made her change her mind about the beating, but in retrospect, I wish she'd just beaten me instead. She sent my brother, Edward out to the corner grocery for a pack of cigarettes. 'So you want to smoke, hey? I'm going to let you smoke.' she said. Nana was furious. 'Why are you going to let that baby smoke? Don't give her any cigarettes!' Of course, Mommy had made up her mind, so that when my brother came back with the smokes, she led us to our tiny bathroom and motioned for us to sit in the tub. Nana was yelling outside the bathroom door and pounding hard on it with her fist. 'Don't let those kids smoke! What is wrong with you!?' But Mommy wasn't listening to her. She was opening the pack of cigarettes and talking to us. 'So you want to smoke, huh? Well here, I'm going to let you smoke. Take one of these.' I took a cigarette and Edward did too. She lit both cigarettes and each of us began to smoke. She lit up one for herself, and we were all three smoking; us in the tub and mom sitting on the toilet seat. Edward said, 'Mommy's great, isn't she, she lets us smoke!' He took a few long drags, coughed, and then laughed through the coughing. I thought she was pretty special myself and nodded approvingly."

Dr. Townes stopped the voice speaking through my mouth. *Thank God*, I thought. My mouth was tired, my throat was parched, and my voice was getting hoarse.

"Did you smoke the entire cigarette?" he asked. His eyes widened, and his brow furled; he was shocked by what he had just heard. I had hoped it was time to leave, and I could stop talking, but now the voice in my mouth felt it had to continue.

"I smoked a whole bunch of cigarettes!" the voice continued. "My mom kept on handing them to me. At first, I thought it was great. After my brother finished smoking about three cigarettes, he got out of the tub, yawned and stretched, then said that he was tired and was going to bed. I was getting tired, too."

Then, the previous voice stepped from behind, replacing the one who had just been speaking. The force behind that voice caused me to sit up straight, raise one eyebrow, and lean forward toward the therapist.

"I smoked an entire pack of cigarettes! My brother brought back two packs but only smoked three cigarettes out of them, and then he left. I smoked a whole pack. My mother only smoked a couple. I was tired, too, and started to get up to leave the bathroom and my mother said, 'Where are you going? You wanted to smoke, didn't you? Well SMOKE.' My mother's eyes seemed to close, but I could still see her eyeballs; like slits with light inside. She looked like the devil."

Dr. Townes was trying to get it all on paper, but the voices were speaking faster than he could scrawl onto his legal pads. I was so frightened by what was happening to me. Who were these voices? I couldn't tell, but they were definitely not the Masculine One. I knew her. I needed to stop talking, but I couldn't stop the flow.

He looked aghast; his mouth was wide open, and he had taken off his glasses with a rip of his hand. He held his glasses on his lap, dangling them from his knee. "What happened then?" he asked, still struggling to write as fast as the voices could speak.

I didn't want to continue. My jaws ached and my throat was extremely dry. I held my mouth shut with my hands but could feel my lips struggling, moving almost mechanically now, up and down, like cogs and wheels and other moving parts, independent of me.

"Get your hands off our mouth!" I finally recognized a voice. It was definitely coming from the Masculine One. Fearing that an onslaught of useless profanity would spew from my mouth, I tried desperately to gain control of myself. I'd had enough. This was complete lunacy. I began to shake my head from side to side, left to right, violently, as though by doing so I could loosen these biddies out from my head, "No! No! No! No more."

The therapist placed his glasses on the small end table beside the wingback chair where he was sitting. He sat next to me on the couch and leaned into my face. "Listen. I don't want to force you to speak about these things right now if they are unpleasant."

Exhausted, I checked the clock that sat on the underside of the end table by the chair. It was 5:30 and my hour was up.

There was nothing even remotely delicious about what was going on anymore, and I wasn't giddy, I was scared, and not at all sure I even wanted anymore to do with this. Nevertheless, I made another appointment and promised to come back.

Chapter Six

Week Five

I entertained the grandchildren over the weekend, which ordinarily would have been filled with fun and frolic for all. I always felt like a little kid when I was with them, but now, I suspected that the Little Me thing inside was having all the fun with them instead. It certainly wouldn't be good if one of the others should do something I didn't like, so I guarded my behavior. It was for a good reason, I thought, and all for the best that I keep my distance for a while. My behavior had become increasingly more inconsistent as I tried to control the ins and outs of these others in my head.

The leaves on the trees along my route to the therapist's office were in deep tones of amber, red, and yellow, so pretty to watch as I drove. The sun was in mid sky, its red glare to my left as I drove north to the office complex. I thought about my day, which hadn't been especially busy, and which was actually not so good for me since it left me plenty of time to mull over the direction my life had gone in during the last month of therapy. There wasn't very much activity with the others in my head, thank goodness.

Perhaps they're all asleep, I thought.

"Fat chance!" one of them blurted. I thought perhaps I'd woken one of them. With so much going on in my head, I figured thinking on the way to the therapist's office might not be such a good idea. As I pulled into the parking lot, a strange sensation caused me park the car well away from the other cars. *Hubby doesn't want dings.* Another strange voice had invaded my mind. It was still early, so I took the key out of the ignition and sat there, hoping not to think anymore.

Just as I was settling in, a strong urge to leave the car suddenly overwhelmed me, and I panicked at the thought of being late. The more I sat there, the more impossible I found it to think about not thinking. My attempt at vegetating my brain was wasting time. I suddenly felt like a stickler for time, so I compromised and waited a few more seconds, until 4:28 exactly. Then I got out of the car, walked into the complex, and sat down in the waiting room.

Dr. Townes was a little late again but wasn't looking as tired and disheveled as in previous visits. I politely nodded when he asked if I was doing all right. He motioned for me to join him.

He began the conversation this time. Today I did not want to be a chatterbox like I was at the previous session. "Will I be going into my Safe Room today, Doctor? You did say that I might." I really liked the Safe Room because I could make things appear and disappear at will and place whatever I wanted in the room.

"Yes," he said. "Let's get started early. I believe more may emerge today, and I'm enthusiastic about meeting them, as I'm sure you are."

He was both right and wrong. By now, I had at least eight voices in my head, sometimes arguing among themselves, and even at times grouping together or ganging up on each other. At times it was difficult to keep my head from exploding. I knew by now that I had only met Little Me, Sick and Tired, Big Fat, and the Masculine One formally, but there were others invading my head.

The therapist began our session the way I had become accustomed to. I became adept at getting to the front yard of the big Victorian house, moving past the large red double doors at the end of the porch. I was familiar with the large round table with the vase that I always made sure was filled with my favorite flowers: freshly cut lavender, lilacs, and gardenias, mostly, the kind that smelled like the perfume I wore. As I opened the French doors, I noticed it was no longer bright and sunny outside. I went to the large bow window and peered out at the sky, which was getting cloudy.

Looks like a storm is brewing, I thought.

Little Me was not in the room yet, which seemed a bit strange, since she always got there before I did.

"Where are you?" asked Dr. Townes.

"In my Safe Room. The sky is cloudy, like it is going to rain."

"What are you wearing?" he asked.

"A pair of black slacks and my black cashmere sweater set." He asked if Little Me was in the room, and I told him I didn't know where she was.

"I believe Little Me does not want to participate today. However, we will to try to encourage her to come into the Safe Room." The therapist tried calling out to Little Me, tried to persuade her to join me in the room. What could possibly have upset her?

"Perhaps it's cloudy outside to reflect how Little Me feels today," I said.

Dr. Townes' voice grew stern and sounded like a parent trying to coax an impudent child into behaving. "Little Me, join us in the Safe Room. We need you in here right now."

I pleaded into the air in the room, hoping she was near enough to hear me. Gradually, a little face, then a little body moved from behind a chair that suddenly appeared in the room to the left of the fireplace. Her cheeks were a bit flushed, as though embarrassed by her behavior. I hugged Little Me, then turned to sit in the chair she brought into the room. Little Me sat on my lap, wiggling her legs to and fro and playing with a ball of yarn that appeared between her fingers.

"I didn't want to come into the room today. I changed my mind and don't want you to meet the Trollop."

My mouth flew open. *The Trollop?* The name alone suggested something seedy. *Do I have something sleazy in me as well?* The thought of ill repute lurking somewhere in my psyche was preposterous. I didn't even like sex. *An obstinate child, a fat slob, a dirty depressive, and a rage filled fireball; what could possibly be next?* I thought, offended by the notion.

"Why don't you invite the Trollop to join you in your Safe Room, Little Me?" asked Dr. Townes.

Little Me abruptly jumped off my lap and reluctantly walked toward the French doors. A presence entered the room. I strained to make out the form. The shadowy figure began to move around, forming the image of a small young woman. As the figure came into better focus, I noticed she was wearing a neat little dress, not too revealing, with strappy sandals on her pedicured feet. She wore a large, floppy hat that hid a great deal of her face. Once she was fully recognizable, the woman hurried to hide behind the couch so that we couldn't see her. I was very curious to find out who she was and wondered what the others thought of her.

"What are you doing?" Dr. Townes explained that he wanted to know if the Trollop was the figure who entered the room. "Who are you?" he asked.

Little Me interrupted. "She's hiding behind the couch. She's afraid to come out. She thinks I don't like her."

The therapist suggested Little Me bring the woman to the large round table in the center of the floor. Little Me obliged and walked over to the woman, who appeared extremely apprehensive, almost frightened to see Little Me so close. Nevertheless, Little Me hugged her tightly and kissed her hat on the wide part of the brim, since the hat covered that part of the woman's cheek that Little Me couldn't get to. Little Me walked slowly with her, reassuring her and holding her wrists with her tiny hands, while the woman stepped lightly, jerking back slightly. They slowly moved forward together, until they both got to the large table in the center of the room.

The woman took off her large floppy hat and set it beside the flower vase on the table. She was very beautiful; young, trim but not skinny, with nice hair, and looking much the way that I always liked to look. She certainly did not look like her name suggested.

Two comfortable chairs matching the one I was sitting in appeared at opposite ends of the table that Little Me had suddenly changed from round to oblong. Once again, Dr. Townes asked the woman to identify herself. The woman looked around the room, and then sat down in one of the chairs. Little Me placed an ashtray on the table for the woman as she lit a cigarette. After taking a long, deep drag of the cigarette, the woman tapped the ashes into the ashtray, at the same time exhaling small tangled loops of smoke into the air.

Then she smiled timidly and spoke. "For years I've been fighting to be understood. First let me say I'm not a slut. Little Me named me Trollop because she likes the sound of it." She took another long, purposeful drag from the cigarette, drew the smoke up from her mouth to her nose, and then slowly blew it out of her mouth.

"The others believe I'm promiscuous," she said through the smoke. But that's because they all hate sex and don't want any part of it. Our husband is a saint, you know? He should have left us a long time ago, because he doesn't get any, which is most likely because nobody else wants to give him any, and frankly I'm just not interested in coming out anymore." The Trollop extinguished the cigarette half way, and then pulled out another.

"To be honest, I don't like sex much, either. Nevertheless, I simply learned how to harness it for strength. It gives me power. I am the boss when I'm out and about. When I use it with a man, I am in command. I decide what I do. I am the one who chooses. Sex is simply used to get started with a prospect, no more, no less. I know what men want. When I walk into a bar, I decide whether I am taking somebody home. I decide if I am going to use sex. Make no mistake, sex is just a tool, something I use to draw a man in, and that doesn't make me a whore, just smart." She smiled, less timidly and more assuredly. "Now, it is true that I have engaged in risky behaviors, but that's one of the reasons I will only come out when we are not married. I'm getting too old for complications."

Townes was silent. I was wondering what he was thinking. The Trollop sounded like a conniver. Her appearance belied her description of herself. *Good Lord*, I thought. I walked over to the large bow window on the right of the fireplace, sat on the window seat, and stared out at the tree to the left of center outside.

The Trollop continued. "I can handle things with the men I get wrapped up with. Our problems start because Mushy thinks that any man I screw, I should start a relationship with. After I have sex with a man, I'm pretty much finished with him. If Mushy steps in, we get into trouble. That is how we ended up with that schizophrenic, John the Baptist, for two and a half years."

I just had to ask, "Who is Mushy?"

Since the therapist didn't respond, I figured he wanted the Trollop to continue, so I didn't repeat the question.

He asked, "Do you want to elaborate on that?"

The Trollop realized I hadn't met Mushy yet and explained. "Mushy is in love with love, just loves everything, even rocks. Here's the way it usually works. Mushy gets involved with someone, falls in love, gets hurt, then backs away. Then Sick and Tired emerges and can only be quieted by doping her down with anti-depressants, which affects us all. A vicious cycle I call it."

As Little Me sat transfixed by the Trollop's smoke rings, I was completely perplexed. Could this all be possible? Was the Trollop the one responsible, back in 1983, right after my first divorce when I brought a man home one night thinking he was fine like Michael Jackson but had actually given me crabs? "Perish the thought!" I said loudly, startling everybody in the room. *But who else could it have been but the Trollop?* I thought. *There were so many occasions when I found myself in compromising situations with men and wondered how in the hell I'd gotten there.*

I wanted to ask the Trollop so many questions and asked Townes if I could. He acknowledged me but stopped short of allowing me to ask her anything. "There will be plenty of time to ask questions, but right now I'd like to hear from the Trollop. "What were your recollections, and when did you think you came to be?"

The Trollop began again. "My earliest recollections are memories of my brother and me eating raw bacon from the fridge. I remember giving the dog a birthday party and feeding him cereal... clothes hanging from the laundry rack in the kitchen over the table... sitting inside the cabinet my father was building... making soup out of dust, water, and candy balls from the candy dish for fun. We lived in New York on Caldwell Avenue. I remember the address. It was 729 Caldwell Avenue."

Dr. Townes asked, "Do you know whether any of the others existed with you at that time?"

"No," she said. "Not that I can remember."

The Masculine One started to fidget in her seat. She got up and began to pace slowly back and forth, from the fireplace to the grandfather clock, which suddenly appeared inside the room between the two sets of French doors. The Trollop stopped briefly to watch the Masculine One, who had hastened her stride back and forth, leaving a cloud of smoke and sparks in her wake.

Undaunted, the Trollop continued. "I believe I may have been the most negatively affected by the way we were raised. Without a father, even though there were males present during my childhood."

"Little Me was raised without a father," said Dr. Townes.

"Oh, I know that," the Trollop said. "But I believe her not having a father affected the choices I made in the kinds of men who got inside, you know?" The Trollop stood up from the chair.

"I really think something needs to be said for the goodness that Mushy really has for people. I didn't care about those men, but if we had let *me* run things, then we wouldn't have the nice husband we have now. He was supposed to be a one-night stand, too, you know."

The Masculine One heard more than she cared to and blurted, "She's full of shit! The only thing the man we have now can claim is that he works and hasn't hit us. That's it."

"I get the feeling you don't like the husband, Masculine One."

"No. But I don't like any of them. I don't think we ever needed anybody."

Dr. Townes asked, "When did you begin to exist?"

The Masculine One paced faster and faster, between the grandfather clock at one end and the fireplace at the other. She was getting more and more agitated, which didn't really take much coaxing, or so it appeared.

"The first time when Little Me got extremely frightened and screamed louder than she ever had before. I could feel her fear and dread. She wanted to scream and fight something heavy and smelly but couldn't move, so she screamed and cried. She said, 'Somebody help me,' so then I kicked, punched, and bit and fought my way out of it. I fought hard and got away. Then I ran home."

The Masculine One punched the air like some prizefighter shadow boxing against a wall. "I didn't really know about anybody else, and Little Me pretty much kept me from coming out most of the time. Only when she was really in trouble and needed me to fight her battles. I met the Trollop first, and the Perfectionist next. After that, it took some time, but I found out about Sick and Tired, Mushy, and the Trollop. Then I stumbled over Big Fat. I met the Gatekeeper last, through this therapy."

Much too quickly it seemed, the angels appeared once again in the four corners of my Safe Room and then Jesus appeared.

"No," I said. "Can't I stay just a few minutes more? There are others, and I want to meet them."

The therapist was already praying, and Jesus was smiling with His arms outstretched. The Trollop walked over to Jesus. He placed his hand on her shoulder, and she smiled, and then disappeared into Him. Little Me was next, eagerly joining the Trollop, disappearing into Jesus. Then the others followed in succession, until only I was left. Finally, I walked over to Jesus and stood in front of Him as He quickly disappeared into me. I left the large Victorian house, noting that the clouds had gone away, leaving the sun alone in the blue sky, high and yellow, warm and bright. It was 5:30, I was back in his office, and it was time to go home.

As I drove the long drive home from the therapist's office, I watched the sun as it followed on my right this time, peaking in and out between the trees along the road, sometimes disappearing between the thick forests and then appearing like an animal prowling for prey. I admired all the beautiful colors of pink, aqua, and a dark gray blue in spots that looked painted by God Himself. I loved looking at the sky while driving, thinking of how I could incorporate those colors in what I would wear in the next few weeks.

Chapter Seven

"D*o you realize?"* A voice in my head asked. I couldn't recognize the voice, but it caught my attention.

"What do you mean?" I asked.

"You didn't get to meet me, but trust me, you will soon. I have a lot to say and don't always get the opportunity to say it. I want you to reflect on what the Trollop said today so we can discuss it. Okay?"

Recollections flooded my mind, like scenes in a movie, but in flashes, one after the other. I pulled the car over to the side of the road and parked. The Trollop was the star of the movies in my head, but the recollections felt like they could have been my own. The voice introduced herself as the "Chatterbox." I always thought I could be overly talkative at times and wasn't really surprised when I heard her name.

The Chatterbox narrated as I watched the time when the Trollop borrowed my mother's car to go out one hot, muggy summer night in 1983 and went to a trendy club in town. I was newly divorced and felt lonely but didn't recall going out by myself anytime during that year. Nevertheless, here she was, alone at the bar, looking like me, sitting on the stool and drinking Heineken and Grenadine, one after another. I wasn't a drinker, and neither was the Trollop, apparently, considering her choice of drink. Perhaps she thought that adding the Grenadine would make that horrid drink somewhat less horrid if it were pink. A little while after she arrived and sat at the bar, a man walked over and offered to buy her a drink. She graciously accepted and ordered yet another Heineken and Grenadine. Looking quite fashionable for the time, the man smiled with a toothy grin and then said he would see her later. She smiled back politely. *No harm*, I thought as I watched intently, intrigued by the vision.

The Chatterbox said the Heineken and Grenadine made the Trollop feel sexy and alluring but alluded to the more plausible possibility that she was drunk. She said the Trollop wanted to dance but intimated that she more likely wanted to show off her pretty figure.

She got up from the barstool and stood very close to the dance floor without actually walking onto it, not wanting to appear too eager to dance. She then moved subtly, sensually, to the sound of the music, gyrating sometimes but not too much, just enough to grab attention from the men on the floor. She eventually accepted a dance from the man who had bought her a drink earlier. He walked over with his arm outstretched, smiling that toothy grin. He wasn't very cute close up, but then, The Chatterbox said, the Trollop figured it was just a dance. He wasn't up for consideration for anything else. The Trollop was confident of that.

After a while, the Trollop began to get annoyed with the pounding bass tones and loud, fast music. Something about those dance songs at clubs and how they droned on and on. The man she was dancing with sweat profusely from his brow, droplets popping off him like so many fleas and landing on her when he got too close. The Chatterbox said the man began to stink. The Trollop was definitely finished with him and politely tapped him to let him know she was leaving the dance floor.

Then The Chatterbox recounted the man's anger upon seeing the Trollop leave the floor. He was standing there, staring at the Trollop as she turned to walk away, and then yelled, "Whadyuu mean?" His eyes grew wide. "This party's just gettin' started!" Then he barked like a dog, "Woof, woof, woof."

The Trollop was completely outdone by now and wanted to get away from him, but he was becoming increasingly unruly. I sat transfixed in the car as I watched the man grab the Trollop by the arm and pull her back when she tried to leave. She was visibly nervous, and although there were people all around the crowded dance floor, no one was paying attention to what was happening to her.

The Trollop tried to walk away again, arguing with the man to leave her alone. Then he followed her from the dance floor and shouted loudly, "I bought you a drink. Whadyuu think that means? That means you're mine for tonight, bitch!"

I was mortified but couldn't help wondering why the Trollop went out alone that night. I would have wanted to disappear. The man began cussing, calling the Trollop an "uppity bitch." The Chatterbox continued to narrate as I watched how people in the club were watching them. The man trailed closely behind the Trollop, yelling and cussing. Some people looked disgusted, as though Trollop and the man were together, a couple of riffraffs having a row in the club. The embarrassment had to be excruciating.

Completely captivated by the visions, I forgot I was parked on the side of the highway. A state trooper pulled up behind me and flashed his lights into my car. He played his siren twice and then proceeded to exit his vehicle. He motioned for me to lower my window, and I did, but just enough that we could hear each other.

"Are you okay, Miss? Do you need an ambulance?"

Still a bit stunned, I hadn't responded to his first question. "Uh, no, Officer, I'm okay. I was feeling a bit tired and pulled over to rest for a while."

The officer asked for my license, insurance, and registration, checked me out, and then allowed me to leave.

The Chatterbox was still in my head, trying to get me to focus on the Trollop and that evening in 1983, but I had to get going. The Masculine One moved into position, took over the wheel, and drove home.

My husband, Victor, was waiting at the door. Apparently, he'd been calling, but I didn't answer my phone. He'd called more than eight times while I was parked on the side of the highway, transfixed on the visions in my head. I tried to assure him I was not sick, just tired, and that he would have to order out for food again. I dragged myself upstairs, got undressed, and fell into the bed.

The Chatterbox was relentless. I closed my eyes and the visions started again. I couldn't tell if I was awake or asleep. I felt fully aware, but my eyes were closed, and I couldn't open them or move my body. She began to narrate from where she left off earlier.

She said that the Trollop decided that the best way to get away from that man was to go into the ladies' room and hide out until he moved on, but before she got to the ladies' room door, another man, small in height but big in attitude and muscles got between them. I watched as the other man asked, "Is he bothering you, Miss? Are the two of you together?" The sweaty, toothy man and the Trollop blurted out opposites, "Yeah, No!" respectively.

"Would you like him to leave you alone?" the man asked the Trollop. She nodded rapidly, wide-eyed and fearful. Then the muscle man with attitude growled, "The lady would like you to leave her alone."

The sweaty, toothy man raised his hand high into the air and then brought it back down as he turned away, waiving them off.

The Chatterbox related that the Trollop felt grateful, and thanked her Lancelot, who rode into the club to save her life from the sweaty, toothy dragon. The Trollop thought he was a nice looking man, although not dressed especially cool. The Chatterbox mentioned that the Trollop was considering Lancelot for a bedding down but wasn't giving him points for his outfit. The Trollop gave Lancelot the once over subtly enough that he wouldn't notice. He was neat, clean, and smelled really good.

The Trollop felt those were attributes that could get Lancelot bedded. He stretched out his arm for her to walk with him to the bar. "Nice, he has manners," the Trollop said as I watched. She sat with him at the bar for a time and laughed at his jokes. She noticed he had a lisp and deducted a point in his overall score. But a lisp was certainly not enough to kick him to the curb. According to the Trollop's scorecard, he was ahead on points.

After a while, the club lights began to flicker off and on, a signal that it was time to leave. Time flew. They walked together to the noisy street with headlights glaring and horns blowing from the nearby parking garages.

"Do you need a ride?" the Trollop asked Lancelot as he walked ahead of her, toward the corner where the bus sign stood.

"Sure, that would be great." he said appreciatively.

Why not? I thought, *he'd saved her, driving him home was the least she could do, right?* The visions continued.

The Trollop pulled my mother's car out of the parking garage, a leased 1983 cobalt blue Datsun 220 hatchback. She reached over to unlock the door on the passenger side, and he got in. They drove to the west side of the city, not far from the neighborhood where I got my first apartment when I was nineteen years old.

They stopped at one of the old apartment buildings that dotted that section of the city. Lancelot said that his apartment was one of them and told the Trollop she could park in front of the building. He motioned to a spot on the street.

As I watched, I was certain the Trollop was going to leave. Certainly, she would just let him get out of the car, would waive politely and then drive off. But then, that was her, not me, and I was just watching what happened, like watching TV.

Lancelot turned in his passenger seat toward the Trollop and kissed her. His breath smelled good and his lips were soft. His tongue was gentle in its approach, at first licking slowly around the outline, his lips moving methodically all over her mouth. Then he gently pried her mouth open with his tongue and explored it like a seasoned voyager but enjoying the surprises of this new exploration.

The Trollop melted into her seat like a pat of butter in a hot frying pan. She leaned in toward him as he finished his kiss, and then he slowly backed away. He reached back in again and kissed her softly once more, just a peck, and then just stared at her.

He asked, "Do you want to come up?"

The Trollop nodded and followed him out of the car into the old apartment building, into the elevator, down the long corridor, and then into his apartment.

As The Chatterbox narrated, images of his small apartment flashed through my mind. It was somewhat cluttered, with papers on the coffee table and a few dirty clothes on his couch. The lamp in the room was dim. There was a clunky old chest of drawers in the living room. On top of the chest were magazines that looked like the usual kind of pornography that men kept.

The Trollop walked over to the chest and then stepped back with a start. A large, rusty butcher knife rested in a pile of pages torn from one of the magazines, its pictures of women being mutilated, some with blindfolds. The handle of the knife was long and dirty, made of brown wood that looked like it had been stained with the blood of so many short ribs, pork chops, and steaks in a butcher shop. There was a magazine near the knife. The title was "Snuffing."

What the hell? I thought. *What did she walk into?* I became frightened for the Trollop and didn't want to see any more of this vision, but The Chatterbox was insistent and continued to narrate while the vision flashed.

With a bottle of cheap, red twist cap wine and two small plastic wine glasses in his hand, Lancelot walked out of the kitchen, sat down on the couch, and motioned for the Trollop to join him. He swiped the papers and some clothes off the coffee table and onto the floor to make room for the wine glasses and wine bottle.

"I have to go to the bathroom," she declared, trying not to show how terrified she was. Lancelot smiled and showed her to the bathroom door.

That man has a butcher knife on the chest of drawers! I thought, frantic about the Trollop's predicament. The Trollop was in trouble, big trouble, and didn't know what she was going to do to get out of it. This man was probably going to carve her up like so many of the pictures from the magazines on top of his raggedy chest of drawers.

I know she got out of it, I'm still here, I thought, trying to console myself as the vision sped past in my head, watching the Trollop in that stranger's bathroom, the one who kissed well, the Lancelot, who saved her from the sweaty, toothy dragon. She finally came out of the bathroom and sat next to him, who by now had stripped down to his clean, white wife beater T-shirt and dingy white boxers.

It was evident from what I saw next that Lancelot wanted to do it. He leaned into the Trollop and pulled her close. Then, at the exact moment when Lancelot unbuttoned the top button of her blouse, she seemed to have an epiphany much like the one I was having. *Give him what he wants or you die.*

Her blouse was soaked from her perspiration, which seemed to arouse Lancelot even more. He unbuttoned the second button more aggressively, all the while kissing her, licking her ears, and sucking her neck until it bruised. He was even more vigorous with his hands on the buttons of her shirt as he worked his way down her blouse, and simply tore off one of the buttons too difficult for him to unfasten. He leaned harder against her body, flattening her on the couch, grinding and heaving his body rhythmically in semi-circular motions, thrusting up and down. He lifted her up slightly to pry her arms out of the sleeves of the blouse. Then he kissed her body more, only pausing slightly to pull off his undershirt, and then falling back down on her as she lay undressed on the couch from the waist up, her bra slung over the dim lamp on the end table near the couch. His lips trailed from the tip of her chin, licking until he reached her breasts. He twirled his tongue over them, around the nipples, and then slowly past. He lightly kissed past her stomach, to her navel, unbuckling her belt. He slid her pants down her legs, then off, and tossed them onto the floor. He slid his face downward, moaning and mumbling. Finally, he met what he wanted with his mouth and drew in like a vacuum cleaner sucking up dirt on a rug. After a time, he covered her with his muscular body, reached down for his penis, and penetrated her.

When it was over, he rose up, smiled, and mumbled, "That was some good shit. I'll be back, gotta pee." He went into the bathroom, closing and locking the door.

Get up and get out of there! I thought; terrified at the prospect of what was ahead of her if she stayed. The Trollop didn't appear to think twice about running away as she grabbed her pants and panties off the floor, her bra off of the lampshade and her blouse, and quietly sneaked out the apartment, closing the door behind her.

She didn't die, I thought. I just kept thinking that since I was still alive, obviously she didn't die.

The Chatterbox continued to drone as I watched the Trollop tipping down the corridor until she found a utility closet with its door unlocked. She hid inside the closet, and with the tiny amount of light from the outside hallway, she managed to get dressed. As she reached for the doorknob to leave, she heard another door open. Footsteps gradually got louder and louder on the wooden floor, as they headed toward the utility closet, growing louder still as they passed the utility closet. Then they headed toward the elevator, down the corridor, came back, and stopped just short of the utility closet.

The Trollop was frozen with fear. The footsteps started again and they drifted away. She heard the sound of a door close behind them. I wasn't able to see who was walking in the corridor, but I imagined it was Lancelot. The Chatterbox finished by telling me that the Trollop remained for a small time in the utility closet, thanking God for sparing her from her own stupidity.

God protects fools and babies, and she was surely a fool, I thought. I couldn't figure out how a woman who said that she used sex as a tool and appeared so much in control in the Safe Room had actually participated in consensual rape.

The Trollop moved The Chatterbox from her perch in front and began to speak. "I didn't consent. The others did and I was overruled. I knew when I went up to his apartment that I was coming for sex. I was in control of the situation until I saw the knife."

The Masculine One chimed in. "The Trollop could have gotten us all killed."

How troubling it was to recount that episode with the Trollop. I really didn't want to see any more of the seedy details. I thought of how happy I would be if she didn't show up for my scheduled therapy session, not even in the Safe Room.

I was finally able to move and opened my eyes, noting that it was about 4:00 a.m., much too early to get up. I tucked the covers around my husband and myself and finally fell asleep.

Chapter Eight

Week Six

Marissa had stopped speaking to me. Of course I knew why. It was because I didn't want to share any the seedy details of my therapy with her. I suspected that she probably knew everything already, because I didn't trust my therapist. He was always talking about his other patients to me, a fact I thought was totally unprofessional, even though he never named names. He was constantly comparing me with some of the real nuts that he kept in his nut jar on his desk, trying to make me "feel the severity of my issues," he would say.

I decided to give her a taste, just enough of the confusion I originally thought was delicious, but not all, not yet. I didn't know whether it was safe to let her know just how utterly insane I was.

I called her, and before I hung up the phone, she was standing in my doorway, eyes wide and hungry.

"Okay, wait, start from the beginning. You've been going for a minute, haven't you? I'm so excited. How do you feel? Is he helping? How do you feel about him now?" She was relentless in her questions, but I couldn't blame her; she had been holding it all in for six weeks. I answered each question, but didn't offer any other information. I told her about the Safe Room.

"Oh, yeah, I've been in there. That's where I found out about most of my issues. How was it for you?" she asked.

I shrugged. "It's very strange." That was going to be all I would say on that subject to her, at least for the foreseeable future.

I pulled into the office complex and parked well away from the trees. When my therapist finally came to get me, it was 4:35. He was in good spirits and excited about the new water cooler with the hot and cold water selections he'd bought for his waiting room, so I didn't have the heart to scold him for being late again.

"Would you like some hot coffee?" he asked. I explained that I was a tea drinker and thanked him, nevertheless.

I began our session by explaining what I saw in my head the week before, a time when I was sure the Trollop had placed my life in danger. I told him that I would just as soon not remember any more stuff like that.

"I believe what you experienced was a flashback," he said, preparing himself for my session. He explained that I would experience many of those, depending on the number of things that were repressed or blocked, and that he would guide me through them as they occurred. I was beginning to think that therapy was a bad idea and that I might have opened up a can of worms.

I entered the large Victorian house, after of course making myself comfortable, fluffing my pillow underneath my head on the couch, and listening to the click, click, click of the clock on the wall, like a metronome keeping time during a music lesson. It was bright and sunny in my room again, not at all as it was the week before. Little Me was playing quietly with dolls on the cushions of the new settee that she created under the large bow window at the right side of the fireplace. The cushions matched the pretty green and white flowered and striped curtains she'd made before.

Dr. Townes asked, "What are you doing?"

I explained that Little Me was playing by herself, and I was sitting at the oblong table in one of the chairs that Little Me had created the week before. Suddenly, the French doors flung open as though a stiff wind had blown into the room, followed by a burst of flames and hot gas. It was the Masculine One, dressed tastefully in a black pants suit, a cream turtleneck sweater, and smart, black, sling-back kitten heals with tassels in the front.

Must she make such a grand entrance all of the time? I thought. She sauntered into the room and sat down on the new, taupe contemporary couch that I'd added to the room while waiting for my therapist.

"Little Me, who is in the room with you?" Dr. Townes asked.

"There's me, and me, and me," she chuckled. "The me that I am, the me that I show people and the me that I sometimes turn into."

From far outside the room but moving toward the French doors was Big Fat, with her thighs clapping together like bursts of thunder in a harsh summer storm. She slowly opened the doors, out of breath, and stopped to rest.

"Big Fat! Big Fat!" squealed Little Me as she jumped into her massive arms and disappeared into the billowy folds. Big Fat moved slowly into the room until she reached the huge chair, which I hastily added to the room for her comfort.

I noted that both Big Fat and the Masculine One entered the room without assistance from Dr. Townes.

"That is a good thing," he said.

Quietly and very unassuming, the Trollop eased into the room from behind the large comfy couch. She sat down, folding her hands on her lap.

"God Forbid! The Trollop is here," I shouted.

Townes noted that the Trollop was in the room but became concerned about my tone. "Why do you dislike the Trollop?"

I reminded him about what had happened to me the week before, and that I was virtually accosted by someone named Chatterbox that I hadn't met. "I evidently flashed back to a time where she almost got me killed!" I shouted, more heated, angrier.

I could see the rage welling up inside of the Masculine One. She jumped off the sofa and headed toward the Trollop, who threw her hands and arms in front of her face in an attempt to shield herself. The Masculine One pointed her finger into the Trollop's face and admonished her for placing all of us in danger that night.

"If I had come out, I would have killed him, then we'd be in jail," she screamed. Peering out of the rolls of fat between Big Fat's arms, Little Me asked the Masculine One to calm down.

Sick and Tired suddenly appeared in the center of the room, looking as though she hadn't washed in days. She was stinky, hadn't combed her hair, and was wearing the same dingy white undershirt and black double knit stretch pants with the elastic waist. She approached the sofa where the Masculine One was sitting.

"Get your stinking ass away from me! You repulse me!" the Masculine One roared.

Sick and Tired quickly turned and moved toward the Trollop, seated on the large comfy couch at the far side of the room. Seeing that the Trollop didn't seem to care where she sat, Sick and Tired plopped down, sliding to the end of the couch to the arm, where she could rest in fetal position with her head in her hand.

I stood by the large bow window next to the settee, staring outside at the large tree slightly to the left of center. I added flowers around the tree, tall purple ones with yellow and white in the middle. Then I folded my arms and looked straight toward the French doors.

There was a commotion just outside the doors. There were voices—with one extremely loud voice speaking well over the others.

Then two of them entered the room and stood still in front of the French doors. A third woman entered the room behind them.

They were two women and one teenager. One of the two women wasn't dressed especially snappy, somewhat ordinary by my usual standards: simple jeans, and a purple crewneck sweater, purple like the color of the flowers I'd added near the large tree earlier. A logo over the right breast contained the letters LRL.

The other woman was dressed in a very prim voile blouse with a small lace peter pan collar, and a cashmere sweater that matched, draped over her shoulders and buttoned at the top.

Impeccable! I thought.

Although a bit less ostentatious than the Masculine One, she definitely looked like she appreciated the finer things. *Perfect*, I thought.

The teenager sported a bob with Chinese bangs spread across her face, just the way I liked to wear my hair when it was shorter. She was in a tank top, jeans, and really cute flat sandals with very thin leather straps over the toes and behind the heel, just the way I liked to wear my sandals.

I suppose there was too much silence for the therapist; of course, since he couldn't see all of the activity going on in the Safe Room.

"Is there anything or anyone in the room now?" he asked. "You haven't been talking for a while now."

I assured him we all were fine—all nine of us, including me. I said, "Three more people have joined us in the room, but I don't know who they are. I suspect that one of them is The Chatterbox."

Dr. Townes said, "That's wonderful. Have Little Me introduce them one at a time for me, please."

Little Me appeared to be lost in Big Fat's lap and was covered between the folds of fat on Big Fat's thighs. Big Fat gently shook Little Me out from between her arms.

Little Me began wiggling her little cola bottle legs, dangling them and pushing herself down to the floor. She walked past the two young women standing by the open French doors and shut the doors behind them. Then she walked around the two women to the teenaged one, who by now appeared agitated and restless.

When she stood face to face with them, she stuck out her tiny finger, twirled it around a bit, and then pointed to one. "This is Chatterbox." Then the other: "This is the Perfectionist."

Little Me then skipped back to Big Fat's outstretched arms, pulling and struggling to get back onto Big Fat's huge lap. "The other girl is 'Seventeen,'" she finished.

Seventeen was quick to speak. "I don't want to stay here. I don't need to be here because I only have one purpose. I only came because I just want to know one thing." Seventeen opened up. "I want to know why you stayed with him!"

I was confused. I had no idea who she was talking about, and felt attacked by her words. Her tone was extremely accusatory. I asked her if she was talking to me.

Seventeen moved into the room and leaned on the couch, which turned from taupe to bright orange whenever she touched it. She came so close to me that her eyelids touched mine, so I knew I had to be the object of her discourse.

"He was nasty, rude to me, and took pills to get high. I didn't even like him, I liked his cousin, but his cousin was going with Sloody and I didn't take my friends' boyfriends like she did."

"Oh, my," I sighed a long, deep sigh and threw my head down. When I raised my head, there she was, as pretty as I could ever have been at that age, wearing a prom gown of silk and taffeta, and carrying a tiny jeweled clutch. "I didn't even go to the prom! You just had to be with him. Do you remember what you did? Well, I do. You and he climbed up on his mother's rickety coffee table and peered at yourselves in the mirror on the wall, as dirty as it was, and posed like you would have if you were at the prom taking your prom picture!"

"But that wasn't me. It wasn't me." I mumbled as a rush of embarrassment covered my face. My body felt fever hot and my face blushed into fiery patches of crimson, not unlike the Masculine One's fiery persona. I felt like I was being called to answer for something especially odious. Seventeen certainly knew she didn't want this *him* in her life but didn't know who kept *him* there.

Obviously she was one of those others in my head who I had to account for. *But what do I say to myself?* I thought. I told my therapist, "I must have done something really stupid. I can remember being seventeen years old, but I don't know what she's talking about."

Dr. Townes asked, "Did she ask why?"

"Well, yes," I said, and then asked him, "What do I say back to her?"

Seventeen stepped slightly away from me. "I want to know just one thing, and then I'll leave. I don't belong here. I am not here to protect anyone. I want to know just one thing." As she spoke, I felt the words come out of my mouth, loudly, outside of the Safe Room.

In a soft, fatherly voice, Dr. Townes asked, "And what is that, young lady?"

She answered, staring directly into my eyes now, "I just want to know why you stayed with him!"

I was at a loss for words. I didn't have an answer. I was convinced I had completely lost my mind. It was 5:35 p.m. and the parking lot was dark when I left the therapist's office.

"This is what it must be like when a person has lost her mind," I mumbled as I drove the long drive back home. I contemplated the notion that my mind quite possibly didn't even belong to just me; that it belonged to at least seven others, eight if I counted myself, crowding my body and crying to be heard.

I parked my car across the street from my house, happy that I managed to get the same spot right around the bend on the sidewalk where it could sit close to the curb. *No chance for dings.*

Another had thought assaulted my mind as I crossed the street and climbed the steps to my front door. When I got inside, I dropped my bag and flopped into one of the chairs in my living room, closed my eyes and leaned my head back into the cushions. Each session, it seemed, brought more questions and fewer answers, with no prospects of finding any soon.

Once again, just like the night I envisioned the Trollop with Lancelot, my body stood acutely still and my eyes were closed, although I still felt aware of my surroundings. The Chatterbox was the narrator again, and my life with my first husband Gilbert flashed before me to the time before we were married, then when we got married, when I apparently left him, left again, left again, and then came back home, until the last time when I left for good. We had good moments and really bad moments. There were times that I didn't remember, but I knew The Chatterbox planned to throw it all out there for me. *Another flashback,* I thought. That is what my therapist called these experiences.

The Chatterbox recalled the Sunday before the Thursday that I had my baby girl. Evidently it was me, since it looked like me as I was crocheting a white blanket, sitting on the floor with my back against one of the loveseats, the one facing the long wall in the living room. I did remember making clothes for my babies to come home in and I remembered that I finished a white dress, although I didn't know why I made a dress. I wasn't clairvoyant and certainly didn't know the sex of the baby I was going to have. The dress and the sweater I made to match the dress were on the wicker chair by the windows in the living room. I was finishing the blanket when my husband walked in, followed closely by my seventeen-month old son, Michael. That was all I could remember on my own. I knew that more had to have happened, otherwise The Chatterbox would have turned off the visuals. I dug in for what was coming next.

I watched as my husband cleaned seeds out from between the dried, crushed marijuana he kept in an old shoe box top. Evidently, he decided that he would clean it in the living room, where there was more light.

Michael stood in front of him and asked, "Whatcha doin', Daalee?"

"Cleanin' joint, son," Gilbert said, apparently delighted with my son's curiosity.

I asked The Chatterbox if perhaps Sick and Tired was the one who experienced these events.

"Yes," she said, as the visions progressed. I began to envision the events unfolding from this new perspective.

Michael drew closer to Gilbert. "Cannabis, weed, marijuana, that's what it's called," Gilbert continued. "Daddy's cleanin' it so the seeds won't pop out and burn nothing."

My son heaved his nose into the top of the shoe box for a closer look. Sick and Tired tried to concentrate on the blanket, mumbling, "Single crochet, three doubles, wrap around, pull through."

Then Gilbert took some of the cleaned marijuana into his left hand and sprinkled it generously across the opened wrapping paper in his right hand. Sick and Tired bit her tongue and tried to ignore Gilbert.

"See, son, this is what you do. You take the weed and you spread it in this paper, like this, see? Then you roll it up, light it, and toke on it." He folded the marijuana into a cigarette, rolling and rolling until it was very tight. Then he licked the tip and continued to roll until the joint was closed. He took the marijuana cigarette into his mouth, where it disappeared for a while, then he pulled it back out with a rolling motion, his saliva sealing it tighter.

The visions continued as I watched my son mesmerized by his father. I cringed at the thought that Michael would admire what Gilbert was doing. As Gilbert reached over to grab the matches on the underside of the shoe box top, he placed the marijuana cigarette between his lips, holding it so that the cigarette dangled a bit, and then struck the match. Michael reached up to grab the cigarette.

"No son, this shit's for grownups." Gilbert sucked in a deep, thoughtful toke, and then allowed the marijuana smoke to rise above my son's head. The smoke billowed and furled, one reaching over to kiss Michael's cheek, like a smitten schoolgirl. With every toke from the joint, more smoke clouds rose over his head, some circling, and others dancing, almost rhythmically. One caught his nose and pinched it, causing him to sneeze, cough, and swipe his small fingers across his face to release its grip. My son began to dance gleefully around the rising smoke clouds as my husband took another deep, determined toke. He continued to smoke the marijuana cigarette, stoking its fiery red gleam with every drag until there was hardly anything left of the paper or the marijuana. He stubbed it out; Michael watching as the clouds disappeared in its smoky wake.

"Aww, man," Michael said, visibly disappointed that Gilbert had finished smoking.

"You see this? This is called a roach ..." Gilbert continued.

Sick and Tired stopped biting her tongue, opened her mouth, and shouted, "Why don't you just leave?"

All of a sudden, the images stopped, and then began again in slow motion.

Gilbert turned slowly and stood up from the couch. "Don't make me fuck you up!" He raised his hand into the air. Although tall and skinny, Gilbert had a huge hand, the kind that could palm a basketball. I'd seen him do it before at the street ball courts. He raised his entire outstretched hand high in the air, voluminous and threatening, in a gesture partly pointing to Sick and Tired. Sick and Tired looked up at it.

"That's my fuckin' son! His voice was frightening to Sick and Tired and Michael. Sick and Tired grabbed Michael and held him closely to her. I recognized the Masculine One's voice as she told Sick and Tired to leave the room, and watched how Sick and Tired ignored her, turning back to her crocheting.

I was astounded by these events, events that I must have blocked out. I remembered that I was nine months pregnant and wanted to finish the blanket to bring my baby home in, because my due date was in a few days, but this event was not familiar. I watched fearfully as Sick and Tired continued to concentrate on the stitches. "Single crochet, three doubles, wrap around, pull through."

Without warning, Gilbert walked over to Sick and Tired and punched her in the face, between the eyes. I watched how Sick and Tired tried to draw her head forward after having it snapped back to the seat cushion on the loveseat by the force of the blow. Her head bounced a couple of times before coming to rest with her chin resting on the edge of the front of her neck.

After she raised her head from her neck, she jumped to attention at sound of Michael screaming, "Mommy, Mommy, Mommy!" and immediately flung the white blanket out of the way of all the blood, thick and gushy, pouring from her nose.

Why did The Chatterbox want me to see these things? It never mattered before that I didn't know these events had occurred. I pleaded with The Chatterbox to stop the visions and she did so for only a moment, explaining that she was just a speaker, not the host. Confused by her statement, I had no choice but to continue, albeit reluctantly, with the flashbacks.

Then the visions started exactly where they left off, with my son in Sick and Tired's arms, running toward the bathroom. Sick and Tired was drying his tears with the part of her white undershirt not soaked in blood, all the while trying to console him, hugging him and whispering in his ear, "Mommy's okay, honey, Mommy's okay."

In the bathroom, Sick and Tired peered into the mirror over the sink. She didn't look like me anymore. She didn't look like anyone. She was unrecognizable, grotesque. Her face was swollen at the point where Gilbert's fist had punched it, dead on, in the center, between the forehead and the eyes, right above the roundest part of the nose, on the bridge. Her nose was bent and pushed up, twisted and leaning toward the left eye. The left eye was swollen almost shut, black, blue and red; a tiny slit revealing a red, bloodshot eye inside. The right eye looked as though it had been pressed inward by a finger, and could open only slightly. As I watched Sick and Tired examining herself, I noticed that her top lip had swollen so badly, it looked very much like raw, pink link sausage before she cooked it for Gilbert's breakfast. The bottom lip appeared to be the only thing on her face that had escaped major damage.

Sick and Tired wanted to scream but had no voice, so she didn't try. She put my son down beside her while she examined her face in the mirror. He clung to her leg, whimpering and wiping snot and tears on her black double knit stretch pants while she washed her face. Gilbert was ranting in the other room and then entered the bathroom abruptly, snatching my screaming, frantic son. Gilbert dragged Michael down the hall toward the living room.

Sick and Tired followed behind Gilbert as he flung Michael into the wicker chair, admonishing him, "Stop that fuckin' cryin'! Look at your mother! She's a mess!" He ranted, "I told you not to fuck with me, I'm the man! I'm the man!" He turned to her, raising that huge hand that could palm her head like a basketball. He was waiving threateningly at her forehead and shouting. "Look at you now!"

Michael stopped crying, but his eyes appeared distant, almost soulless. Sick and Tired just stood there, helpless to save him. Then after a moment or two, Michael looked at Sick and Tired and then looked at his father, looked at her again and then tried to slide down the chair with his tiny body toward her. Gilbert grabbed him by both his arms and hurled him back into the wicker chair, shouting for him to stay put. Sick and Tired pleaded with Gilbert to allow Michael to come to her but prayed that he would not try to slide out of his chair again on his own. God must have answered her prayer because my son never left the chair until Gilbert stormed out of the house.

The visions stopped, and I could move again. As I sat up in the chair, about to rise, I suddenly had an epiphany, and said, "I had my baby girl on the Thursday following that Sunday. That's why my eyes were bloodshot with black circles around them that day."

"What doesn't kill you ... makes you crazier!"

Chapter Nine

Week Ten

Over two months into my therapy and I was thankful I'd had no flashbacks for about a week. We hadn't been in the Safe Room for what seemed like years and I was a little anxious about the prospect of returning there. Nevertheless, the therapist seemed more interested in discussing my day, my husband, children, and my mother. Today, however, I felt like going into the Safe Room. I was happy to learn that the therapist felt the same way because there wasn't much more about the family that I cared to share. When I got to the Safe Room, the furniture had been removed. There were no pretty green and white flowers and stripes adorning the large bow windows. There were shutters instead, wooden ones, blocking the sunlight.

Little Me was there when I got there, but she seemed disturbed, angry. Her arms were folded around each other and she wore a pronounced pout.

Dr. Townes asked, as he was accustomed to asking since the beginning of my therapy, "Where are you?"

"I'm in my room," I said, "but somebody took everything out and took down the curtains." I suspected that Little Me had changed the room and wondered why she was behaving so unpredictably.

Dr. Townes asked, "Little Me, why do you suppose your room has changed?"

Little Me shrugged, her arms still folded around each other and her lips still poked out. I tried to add a chair, a couch, anything to sit on but I couldn't, which was strange since I could manipulate things in the Safe Room before.

Then he asked, "Little Me, why don't you ask the others to join us?"

Little Me turned to face the large bow window on the left of the fireplace but didn't respond.

I said, "Little Me is being obstinate, Doctor. She's angry about something and won't speak."

The therapist's voice turned into its stern, fatherly voice, explaining that Little Me was *blocking.*

Why was she being so difficult today? I was finding it hard to like her much today, especially with the day I'd had at work with the Albatross, who also behaved very much like a spoiled, impudent child most times.

I asked, "Don't you want to come to your room today?"

Little Me didn't answer.

I tried to coax her with the promise of candy, if she at least allowed Big Fat to join us. She didn't budge. By now she was at the large bow window on the right, peering out through the slits of the dark brown, wooden shutters. I grew annoyed with Little Me. Didn't she realize that this therapy was for me? I knew she changed the room, and she did it because she was angry. But why was she being so stubborn?

At the very least, I was hoping to see Seventeen because I knew the answer to her question now. I wanted to tell her that Sick and Tired was the one she should have asked, that Sick and Tired would have told her she simply hadn't learned how to get away from Gilbert, that Little Me hadn't created someone for that purpose.

Little Me's behavior was decidedly erratic. "Little Me, won't you at least let Seventeen come into the room, so I can answer her question?" I pleaded. She was in charge, I knew it, and wasn't happy about it at all. I pleaded with her again, while she sat, still peering through the slats. I gently touched her shoulder, and she turned with a start.

"I'm mad because you don't want to know anything. You started it and now you don't want to know the truth about anything. You shouldn't have started it," she shouted. In that instant, I thought I could see the weight of her world on her shoulders, and it frightened me to death.

I informed the therapist that Little Me was demanding that I learn everything right away. She was tired of the "back and forth," and that since I asked for it, she wanted to let me have it. I placed the fingernail of my index finger into my mouth and began to chew on it, tearing away at the small amount of nail hanging from it. I knew I'd started this thing, but soon realized that I couldn't remember events for a good reason.

Perhaps I shouldn't remember, I thought. *Maybe I bit off more than I could chew. Wasn't it enough that the others remembered their issues?* I accidentally bit the nail down to the quick.

I apologized to Little Me. After all, it was me who started this thing with the therapist. Just as the Masculine One said when I met her, everything was fine before I embarked on this journey. Little Me was quick to smile and forgive me.

I let the therapist know that Little Me was ready to cooperate, and he asked Little Me to take me by the hand. "Look for the door at the far right of the room, nearest to where the fireplace stands," he said. I explained that the fireplace was gone.

"Look for the door. Look for the white, wooden door on the far right of the room. Do you see it?" he asked.

Suddenly, there was a large door, from ceiling to floor, clean and white, with a huge brass knob, shaped like a clenched fist. Little Me took me by the hand and led me to the door. I hesitated, afraid to open it.

"Open the door," said Dr. Townes, "and walk through the hallway."

Little Me opened the door for me; I was too frightened. She led me into a long hallway, dimly lit by a couple of yellow light bulbs spaced on the ceiling.

"Tell me how many doors you see there, and where they are located," Dr. Townes said.

There were four doors, I told him. There was one set of French Doors straight ahead, with a small amount of light coming from behind them. There was one door on the left wall, and three doors spaced apart, on the right wall. I stopped in the hallway and didn't want to walk any further.

"Little Me, I would like you to pick a door in the hallway and enter it." Then he said to me, "Don't be afraid, you are still safe. Allow Little Me to guide you through the door."

I reluctantly walked with Little Me through the door that was on the left wall of the dimly lit hallway, and we were outside. The surroundings were familiar. I was on Federal Street, on the corner of my block, standing next to Ray's Cleaners on the southwest corner. Dr. Garrell's Drug Store stood on the northwest corner, the beer garden on the northeast corner, and the restaurant on the southeast corner. As I surveyed the old neighborhood, I couldn't help feeling a bit nostalgic. *What a great neighborhood I'd lived in,* I thought.

The neighborhood was bustling with family businesses and nice people. My immediate neighbors, Mrs. Loochi and Mr. Challie, were Italians. I learned how to say their names by the way they called each other. She would yell his name, "Challie!" and he would yell back "Oh, Loochia!" They were very nice to us. During holidays, Mrs. Loochi would make us a huge bowl of spaghetti filled with sausages and gigantic meatballs. When my brother and I played outside in our tiny backyard, Mrs. Loochi would lean over the fence with some delicious cookies that looked like flat waffles, and some other really hard ones, shaped like the letter "S." It was so nice recalling the old neighborhood as we stood between the four corners of my old block.

Little Me directed me across the street on Federal next to the laundromat on the left of a vacant building. Then we walked toward Mr. Peace's store in the middle of the block, next to the church where my mother used to send us for Sunday school. I recalled that Mr. Peace's store carried the best penny candy and chips. There were all kinds of toys, like jacks, paddleballs, and puzzles. My mother always bought hair ribbons and rubber bands from Mr. Peace, and if we got straight *A*s on our report cards, she took us to Mr. Peace's store to get our rewards.

I felt apprehensive as we moved closer to Mr. Peace's store but didn't know why. What was Little Me doing? I began to feel queasy when we stopped at the door.

"Don't go in there!" I shouted. "Don't go in there!" I pleaded with her, but she was shaking my hand and beckoning me to follow.

"Don't be afraid," said Dr. Townes. His voice changed into concerned reassurance, but I detected a tinge of uneasiness that made it impossible for me to calm my fears. "Remember, Little Me is with you, and she is the best part of you."

That was a ridiculously small consolation! I thought, mainly because she was a kid. "How is a kid supposed to protect me?" I asked.

Dr. Townes didn't respond.

I cautiously walked up the stairs that led to the heavy door of the store with Little Me. I noticed the sign above the door, *Peace Confectionery Store*, and could tell by looking through the glass window that nothing inside had changed. It was still kind of dark, very cluttered. Toys were stuffed in cubbies or on the floor, where children had played and left them. Ribbons dangled by nails from the walls, so Mr. Peace could unravel them to cut just the right amount for his customers. There were the candy bins, with all of the candy any child would ever want to have. Then I saw the long, glass front counter, with the good candy Mr. Peace kept behind its thick glass windows: the wrapped candy, and the chips, pretzels, and pixie stix.

I entered the store and inched my way past the first counter, and noticed the opening to the back. Mr. Peace's dented metal stool with the old warped wooden seat stood in the way. I always bumped into that stool when Mr. Peace let me go behind the counter to pick out one of the good pieces of candy or one of the good toys. Little Me stood at the opening in the middle of the floor between the two long counters.

All of a sudden, there was a rumbling in the back of the store, like someone was moving something out of the way. Mr. Peace, who entered the store from the back of the building, startled me. He was still fat and had a big, wide face with a very large stomach. He wore big, dirty brown pants, too big for him, even though he was so huge. He wore a thick, black belt, pulled so tightly that his huge stomach hung over it. He had a flat behind, strange for such a fat man, and his eyes were shifty slits. I stared at him as he walked past me. He didn't acknowledge that I was there, and it appeared he couldn't see me.

He was smiling now, because he'd caught sight of Little Me. He said, "Hi there, sweetie. And what can I do for you, today?"

A cold chill entered my body and made me shiver, even though it was warm in the store. I watched Little Me smile back at Mr. Peace and tell him that she was there for some candy. He said, "Come on back here and get some of the good candy."

"No!" I screamed. Fear rushed through me again. I was getting more and more anxious with every step Little Me took past the stool at the opening toward the back of the counter, where all of the good toys and good candy were kept. She was smiling gleefully as she leaned into the case. She didn't seem to mind when Mr. Peace placed his hand on her shoulder and rubbed it gently, but I felt like a knife had plunged into my chest, and I was finding it extremely difficult to breathe.

Little Me stood up from the candy case and faced toward the opening again to leave, but Mr. Peace blocked her way, sitting on the stool.

"What is he up to?" I asked. I didn't get a response. I tried to move toward Little Me to grab her away but was unable to. My body was frozen in place. I couldn't scream. I couldn't close my eyes. I couldn't do anything but watch what was unfolding before me.

Mr. Peace had taken Little Me and wrapped her arms around themselves so she could not escape his grasp. Everything seemed to be happening so fast, it was hard for me to comprehend anything except sheer terror. I was terrified for Little Me, who was wiggling and writhing, trying to get free from Mr. Peace's grip on her tiny body. Where were the other customers? Why was the store empty except for the two of them?

"She's only four years old!" I screamed. No one responded. Where was the therapist? I pleaded with Dr. Townes to pull us back into the safety of the Safe Room. My mind was the only thing allowed to move, it seemed, whirling like the blades of a helicopter, moving too fast now. I was trying to take it all in; trying to keep up.

Mr. Peace had a vise grip hold on Little Me. Then he plastered his flat, wide, nasty lips all over her tiny face. She stopped moving and appeared limp. I didn't know if she was dead or alive. I felt faint. "Fade to black," I screamed. "Fade to black."

When I finally awoke, I was in a puddle of perspiration on the therapist's couch. He told me that he had to remove me from the situation because I screamed that I couldn't breathe while violently heaving up and down on the couch. He said that he brought me out of the room because it appeared that it might not have been time for me to learn the truth; that he should have trusted his own instincts instead of allowing Little Me to dictate when I was ready. He explained that he would not do that again, but that when I was ready to learn what happened to me, we would go back. Sweat poured off me. My blouse was damp and clammy, and I had to pee.

Exhausted, I got into my car for the journey home. On the way home, The Chatterbox said something strange but curious to me. It was bizarre because I had never thought of it before, and curious because of its nature. She told me to ask the therapist the question at my next session.

Chapter Ten

Week Twelve

I was in my twelfth week of therapy; Townes called it a milestone. He appeared eager to begin our session. I was there on time, as usual, and he was on time for a change. He started right in, taking me into the Safe Room. Although two weeks passed since my last Safe Room visit, I still hadn't asked the question that The Chatterbox told me to ask. Today, though, I thought that it was safe to ask.

"The Chatterbox wanted me to ask you why I never knew when my hymen broke. I thought it was a rather strange thing to ask you, since I never really thought about it, but I am assuming that it is because of what happened with Mr. Peace and Little Me."

Dr. Townes asked me if I thought I was prepared to find out. I certainly wanted to know, after waiting for two entire weeks and having to listen to The Chatterbox's persistent yammering in my head, but I felt it wasn't for me to decide.

"I think we'll be able to clear up any repressed memory of Mr. Peace today," he said reassuringly.

I was accustomed to my Safe Room by now, although I thought that calling it "safe" was a blatant misstatement, considering what had happened.

He asked me where I was, and I let him know that I was planted firmly in the room. "That's good," he said. "Now, I would like to speak with Little Me."

Little Me was playing quietly at her favorite spot, sitting on the window seat by the large bow window on the right side of the room and smelling the fragrant flowers that grew along its borders. The therapist asked Little Me why she went to Mr. Peace's store.

"Well, I liked to go to the store to buy chips and candy and Burley sodas, the kind without the bubbles, because Mommy wouldn't let us drink the bubbly kind. Mr. Peace's store was close by and Mommy allowed me to cross Federal by myself. Sometimes I didn't have money, but Mr. Peace never seemed to mind. I thought he was a nice man, because he let me go behind the counter where the good candy and the good toys were."

I cringed. "Didn't she remember what he did to her three weeks ago?" I felt angry that she was talking as though nothing happened.

Dr. Townes then asked Little Me a pointed question. "How often did he let you go behind the counter to get what you wanted?"

"Oh," she began, "all the time." She bit her fingernails and grinned nervously, perhaps because she thought she shouldn't have done so.

"*Now come here and give me my candy*!" Little Me blurted in a deep and alarming voice. Her demeanor was disquieting and her behavior was more irregular, unusual even for the Safe Room. Little Me grabbed herself and held onto herself tightly. At the same time I couldn't move and felt like I couldn't breathe, a similar predicament I'd found myself in during the other Safe Room visit.

The lights in the Safe Room abruptly turned off. The only light came through shutters that suddenly appeared. Little Me smashed her hand onto her lips, flat handed; pushing and pushing her hand on her face and lips, rubbing her face with her opened palm, rubbing and smashing all over her face until it bruised. She fell onto the floor in the middle of the Safe Room, her hands behind her, as though tied, and began to kick into the air, kicking and screaming. She heaved up and down, back and forth, screaming, "Somebody, help me!" Then she cried, "I have to pee, I have to pee!"

I tried to run over to her and hold her tightly in my arms, to comfort her, but couldn't. She writhed around on the floor for a time, and then she stopped screaming, kicking, and shaking. She laid completely still on the floor, soaked in her own urine. I struggled to move and fell toward her, managing to land just left of the puddle of urine and away from Little Me, and then crawled over to her, cradling her in my arms.

The therapist said, "Ask Little Me to explain what she was doing."

Little Me was calm now, but I was still a wreck and didn't want to stir things back up. "No, I don't want to. She's obviously shaken," I said. "She peed herself. Can I come out of the room, now?" I repeated twice.

"No one can hurt you in your Safe Room. You both are safe," Townes reassured me.

"I think I know what happened," I told Little Me. She rested her head on my chest as I cradled her in my arms. When we stood up, her dress and panties were dry, and there was no longer any puddle of urine on the floor. The furniture and pictures were back now and the shutters were no longer blocking out the bright sun that poured into the room from the large bow windows. Little Me turned and looked up at me, wide eyed and feeling in especially good spirits.

"Mr. Peace," she began, "Mr. Peace grabbed me and held me down, and then he tried to put his nasty pee pee in me. I screamed but nobody could hear me. I couldn't breathe because he was so heavy on top of me. I was so scared that I peed on myself. The Masculine One came out and saved me. She kicked him and bit him on his hand, and kicked him in his pee pee and made him get off of me. The Masculine One carried me to the door, and then she told me, 'Get the hell out of there, NOW!' so I did. I ran and ran, but I kept looking back to see if he was coming after me, but he wasn't. I got home and tried to tell my Mommy, but there was something happening there, and every time I tugged at her dress, she shooed me away. When she finally looked at me, she got mad at me and yelled, 'What did I tell you about waiting to the last minute to go to the bathroom! Look at you! Go upstairs and change out of those wet panties!'"

I had another epiphany. *That's why The Chatterbox asked about my hymen*, I thought. *It broke back then when Little Me was raped and the Masculine One saved her.*

The therapist placed the four angels around the four corners of the room and then Jesus appeared. Smiling gleefully, Little Me ran to Him and hugged Him. He kissed Little Me on her forehead, and then she disappeared into Him. I staggered over to Jesus and fell to my knees. Jesus placed His hand upon my head, prayed silently over me, and then disappeared into me.

When I left the therapist's office for the drive home, I began to pray softly, so thankful to be alive, so thankful to have lived through a trauma like that, and thankful that for the first time it seemed like I made a breakthrough in my therapy.

After learning of the rape, I became very weepy, crying for no apparent reason and not able to sleep. *Running home from Federal Street wasn't a nightmare,* I thought. The others were clamoring inside my head, each with their own idea of what my problem was. Worse still, it appeared that Sick and Tired was making her way to the front more and more frequently, and I found it difficult to control her movements.

Normally, during my workday, I could handle the Albatross. But nothing about me was normal, I thought, and I suspected that somehow, she detected my weepiness, and tried to seize on it at very specific times during the day. At staff meetings, at project meetings, and anytime we were around our boss, it was increasingly more difficult to keep my eyes from tearing up from the simplest of altercations with her. I found myself rushing away to the bathroom, or slipping back to my office for a good half an hour cry before I could return for more sparring. At home, I picked fights with my husband and used our arguments to keep from cooking meals, having sex, or doing anything I knew he found pleasure in.

I explained my feelings to Dr. Townes. His response was that I should take medication, and prescribed meds for me, "To help you cope." I was extremely ambivalent about having to take meds again. I knew they were necessary, even though I didn't really want to go back to taking them. I explained that I used to take two hundred milligrams of Zoloft and ten milligrams of Clonazepam a day. It was during a time when I had a panic attack for no apparent reason.

It wasn't apparent at the time, anyway, I thought. I was subsequently diagnosed with clinical depression. And of course, until the therapy, I thought I was well past that. At that time, I was having trouble with my job, and I thought Victor was cheating on me.

Now I was being asked to take medication again. How I hated the prospect, but Dr. Townes insisted, since he was confident it would help me get through certain rough patches that lay ahead. *Just fifty milligrams of Zoloft this time, with five milligrams of Trazodone to help me sleep.* I thought.

I continued therapy for the next few weeks, but Townes wouldn't put me into the Safe Room. I was annoyed by his seemingly insatiable craving to pry into my everyday personal activities outside of the Safe Room but understood that it was a necessary intrusion, in order to get the complete picture. He kept mentioning Little Me, referring to her as the best part, and I couldn't help being somewhat jealous of her, if something like that was even possible.

Chapter Eleven

Week Twenty

I was both anxious and excited about my visit today. I was finally going to officially meet more of the people swirling around in my head. I immediately made myself comfortable on the therapist's couch and positioned myself in my customary relaxed position, clutching the teddy bear.

Dr. Townes began by talking about my prior sessions and explained that the breakthrough I made over the past five months would help me to get through the other things I would be facing.

"Other things?" I sat up, nervously chewing what was left of the nail on my right index finger. "Wasn't the fact that Little Me was raped at such a young age enough?" I asked. "What other things are you referring to?"

"I'm not going to minimize the trauma from the rape. That was a *tremendous* trauma, no doubt about that, but I am certain there is more to learn." He assured me that I would come out a winner after all was said and done.

When I entered the large Victorian house, it was filled with the sounds of all the voices that I recognized from prior sessions. As I walked through the French Doors to the Safe Room, they were all waiting for me. There was the Masculine One, as angry as usual, and Big Fat, still boisterous, but in a good way. Sick and Tired was being miserable, but managing to muster a tiny smile above her perpetual frown. The Trollop was sitting on the settee by one of the large bow windows, quiet and unassuming.

Little Me seemed happiest of all in the room, dancing around the large round table that she had just put back into the center. She stopped to smell the fragrant, purple lilacs she placed in a vase on the table.

"Lilacs are my favorite flower in the spring," I said to Little Me, pleased to know that Little Me really liked them as well. Dr. Townes asked Little Me to bring back the people who had joined us earlier but were not formally introduced. One by one, three women entered the room through the French doors and stood next to the fireplace where a warm fire had just begun. Two of the women sat on the cushy couch that Little Me had placed back into the room. The third woman found a seat near Sick and Tired.

"This is Mushy." Little Me smiled widely as she pointed to the woman sitting next to Sick and Tired. "She is the Perfectionist, and she is The Chatterbox." She pointed at the other two.

"Where is Seventeen?" I asked Little Me. I wanted to tell Seventeen that I finally knew the answer to her question so she could disappear the way she wanted to.

Sick and Tired answered, "Seventeen won't be back. She understood that it wasn't you and knows her answer."

The Perfectionist sat poised and demure. She looked like the finest demitasse china, delicate and precious. She had not one hair out of place, not one wrinkle in her clothing, and she smelled like my favorite perfume.

Dr. Townes spoke to her first. "Hello, Perfectionist. Would you please tell us something about yourself?"

The Perfectionist crossed her legs at the calves, forming a tiny cross with her feet. She folded her hands on her lap and leaned up slightly, posture perfectly proportioned. Then she spoke softly, "I like order. I like to be in control."

The room became silent, in part because of how softly she spoke, in stark contrast to some of the others in the room. I felt at ease as she spoke. She was soft spoken, just the way I liked to be. She wasn't the loud person everybody always told me I was. I liked her.

"I am glad that I aspire to perfection," she began. "I'm level headed enough to know that I am not going to achieve true perfection, but as long as I'm alive, I will strive to be the best possible, for all of us. This is who I am. I need things to be just so, clean, right, tidy. I don't need to be loud to get my point across. I am self-assured." Her voice resonated with such a cool, quiet confidence that whispered total command of herself and her surroundings. The Perfectionist and her self-assured attitude intrigued me, and I wondered if perhaps I could really have something like her inside me, too. I was convinced that she was responsible for pushing me to pursue my degree after thirty-two years of procrastinating.

The Perfectionist began to talk about my former husbands, which led me to believe that for at least that time in my life, she'd been there. "Our first and second husbands didn't like me very much; called me 'Ms. Perfect.' I used to take offense to that, but not anymore. They were both slobs and losers.

"Gilbert was the nastiest one. I remember when we gave birth to our daughter and got back home after four days in the hospital, I had to clean out the bassinet before I could put the baby inside." Her voice raised slightly, just one octave above her original whisper.

"There were four days worth of crud to clean up, from the kitchen to the bedrooms. I had to work fast, because Sick and Tired was waiting in the wings, ready to jump in, which of course would have been disastrous because nothing would have been done." The Perfectionist turned to Sick and Tired, who nodded affirmatively, agreeing with the assessment. The Perfectionist continued, "I had to blow the whistle on her for a time out, just so I could clean."

Dr. Townes then asked the Perfectionist about her feelings for Sick and Tired, and the others. I sat stone-faced and was somewhat concerned that the

Perfectionist might offend someone, especially the Masculine One or Sick and Tired.

"Sometimes things get extraordinarily coarse, and I have to step in order to make sure that situations don't get unhealthy for us. If it wasn't for the medication, I would be overruled and nothing would be done. The others vacillate, waiting for months before they realize that no one will wash our behinds, or clean our surroundings. I make sure that we keep our cool and keep us from saying stupid things. Since the medication, I can get what I want most times, but on those occasions when the others are dithering, Sick and Tired will slide in and won't wash, sometimes for days. That simply makes me want to jump out of our body!"

Dr. Townes cautioned that time was fleeting, and we had to meet the rest before the session ended. He asked to speak with Mushy, who was a pretty, slight woman, dressed in a bouquet of assorted, fragrant flowers that were shaped ingeniously in the form of a dress. I smiled to myself, remembering how magical the Safe Room was.

"I don't have much to say," Mushy began. "I'm really just someone who loves everything." She looked adoringly at Little Me, who was behind her on the couch, sniffing the flowers that made up her dress, and picking a few to give to the group.

"I'm happy most of the time, and I can find goodness in the smallest things," she continued. "Sometimes I get scolded by the others because they think I am unrealistic. They say that I need to stay away from Sick and Tired and the Trollop, especially the Trollop because when we work together, we get everybody else into trouble with men. I won't elaborate here, because I'm sure that most of what I've done will come out now, since we are being called out. Nevertheless, I am the one who likes nothing but good things, I love being happy and in love. This is just the way I am. Little Me and I agree that we like to be in love. We gush when we see our husband Victor because we love him so much, even if the others could not care less about him."

Townes asked, "You say you and Little Me love your husband. Why do you think the others don't share your feelings?"

One could hear a pin drop in the room as we all listened for her answer. Mushy said, "There are those of us, who I won't name, who only tolerate him, and a few who just don't trust him at all and want me to get rid of him. As long as Little Me and I trust him, he will be with us. I stick close to Little Me so that the others won't try to convince her that Victor isn't worth keeping."

The Chatterbox jumped off the couch, put her hands on her hips and interrupted Mushy. "Okay, why did I get chosen last? What kind of crap is this? I don't mean to be crude, but I have been waiting patiently for months, and I have a busy schedule." She stood up and walked around the round table in the center of the room, popping her head and waiving her index finger into the air as she spoke.

"There are things that I need to get done, and I was here the last time and didn't get to say a damn thing. Oops, I didn't mean to curse, but I do need to get some things off my chest as much as the others do. I didn't get a chance to say anything, which is why I blurted out some things on the way home a few weeks ago."

The Chatterbox rattled on. "I'm the one who talks to Little Me about things. We need someone to keep everybody informed of things—matters of importance, anything, and nothing, just whatever comes to mind. That's my role: information. If I need to say anything else, I will, and I will tell on any of us if I feel that Little Me needs to hear it. I'm the one who warns and the one who knows it all. I'm the one who studies and researches. I'm the one aware of it all, and I don't mind talking about it to us to make sure that we stay informed. Just because I'm smart, and a bit talkative, I'm not taken seriously. But, and this *but* is bigger than Big Fats; don't think for a minute that I won't blurt it out if I have to. That's right! If it weren't for me, we would never have gone back to school to get our degree. I'm the one working the hardest for our success."

Oh, I thought. *She's the one who pushed me back into school.* The others were listening intently as The Chatterbox's voice fluttered and buzzed like the wings of a bee, landing lightly on each person in the room and stinging some wherever it could.

"I know I don't have much time here, but I will say that I for one am glad that I am finally getting a chance to speak what's on my mind. I'm glad I'm getting a chance to tell it like it is. Here it is. Here I am. You will be hearing from me!"

Just in time, it seemed, Jesus appeared in the room. The four angels smiled in their four corners of the room, protecting all of us as one by one, each disappearing into Jesus. Finally, Jesus walked over to me near the large round table and disappeared into me, as He did each session. I felt at ease when I returned to the therapist's office. Townes explained that the session had been a truly productive one, and I had to agree with him for a change. Before I left, he increased my meds from fifty milligrams to one hundred.

Five months were behind me and now, and according to the therapist, I had made tremendous progress toward healing. Now, I was very eager to learn as much as I could about all of the others, since doing so would allow Little Me to mature, and hopefully I would get well. I thought I could be content with that.

Chapter Twelve

Week Twenty-One

Contentment was a coveted treasure, usually fleeting much too quickly before I could savor any of it, since therapy began. One of the things that still gave me pleasure despite my mental condition was shopping. After my session, I decided to hit one of my favorite shopping haunts in order to spend money I really didn't have. The complete and utter pleasure of prowling the aisles, sneaking peeks at the expensive price tags, and secretly calculating how much I could afford to spend was addictive, but I didn't care. I bought a lovely man-tailored suit for the Masculine One, a couple of dainty sweaters for the Perfectionist, flowers for Mushy, gossip magazines for The Chatterbox and of course, white chocolate truffles for Big Fat. There wasn't anything I could buy that would please Sick and Tired so I didn't bother, and I didn't care much about what pleased the Trollop.

I went home with my bounty, pleased with myself, and admiring my beautiful new clothes, hanging the suit in the closet. I carefully folded and placed my sweaters neatly into my sweater drawers. I placed my beautiful flowers into a vase and then headed for bed. I popped a couple of truffles—just two—and then closed my eyes. At least for a moment, I didn't have to think about just how crazy I was.

In the morning, I combed the Internet for more information on my condition; it was all just too confusing to understand. The time drifted past so quickly that I didn't realize I was almost late for my appointment. I let the Perfectionist dress me in a cream, lace-collared blouse. At her suggestion, I pulled my hair into a French twist, tightly secured by bobby pins that I kept in the vanity drawer. My crisp black pants were creased and fell neatly on my bottom half. Her choice of the black cashmere cardigan was indeed a good one. “Perfect,” she said, as I checked myself in the mirror.

I hurried to the office and sat in the waiting room; I had just made it by 4:30, my appointed time. I smiled, thinking the therapist was probably going to be late by least ten minutes anyway, and then the Perfectionist would most certainly comment on his tardiness with a quip; one that I would more than likely have to apologize for. Surprisingly, the therapist was only two minutes late, and I managed to stifle the Perfectionist. “Just two minutes,” I said, “doesn’t deserve a snide remark.”

I arrived at the Safe Room and immediately noticed that Sick and Tired had placed a sign on her forehead that read, “Please, No More Medication.” She was apparently feeling especially put upon because of the meds. “My life sucks. Why me? Langston had it right. No crystal stair! Why are we here? This is only going to get worse.”

I had always wondered about the whisper in my head reciting just that part of the poem, “No crystal stair, no crystal stair.” In fact, I made the words into a screensaver and wallpaper at work and never understood the fascination I had with them. Now I knew it was Sick and Tired who loved to recite it, repeatedly. She used the crystal stair as a metaphor for her tragic life. Funny thing was, I was certain I’d never read the poem, and she probably hadn’t read it either. Nevertheless, Sick and Tired used those words as her personal mantra, her soul identifier. For me, though, they were a pain, the kind of pain that radiated from my inner shoulder, between the bottom tip of my neck and the spread of my collar bones, from left to right. The words aggravated me so much as they slithered up and down my spine to my brain and then back down to where they pressed in the first place, leaving me with nothing more than an empty ache and no explanation of the meaning. Having a life with no crystal stair was Sick and Tired’s reason for her miserable existence. *Yet another epiphany*, I thought.

Sick and Tired turned to me, shaking her index finger wildly, and said, "Listen, I'm thinking that we need to put the dirty laundry back into the bags and run. You just had to get rid of our collective baggage, didn't you! This is your entire fault! No crystal stair for me; never was, isn't now, and never will be."

"What the fuck is wrong with you today, you dumb cluck! Straighten up and take that ridiculous sign off!" It was clear that the Masculine One had no patience for Sick and Tired today. She believed Sick and Tired was making a plea for attention, and a display such as this might persuade the others to ask the therapist to discontinue the medication.

I explained to the therapist that Sick and Tired was having a bad time with the medication, "But it shouldn't keep us from continuing the session." I said.

Dr. Townes began, "Today is a very important day!" He explained that we would begin a series of explorations through the Victorian house. After having taken a little trip through one corridor previously, I was a bit ambivalent about that prospect, since the last time I'd ended up finding out that Little Me had been raped by Mr. Peace. The things I had repressed until now were already very unpleasant.

"I don't want to leave the Safe Room if the other parts of the house aren't safe," I said. The others nodded affirmatively.

"Which is why," Townes reassured, "you need to stay on the medication for now." He assured us that the meds would help all of us cope through some of the twists and turns that these explorations would take. Sadly, it seemed that there was no consolation for Sick and Tired, who retreated into a fetal position in the corner of the couch.

Little Me was asked to take me by the hand. I was told that I could choose someone to go with us on our expedition.

"Will I need to fight?" I asked, knowing that if I had to fight, I definitely wanted the Masculine One with me. Dr. Townes told me that any of the others could come into the room if I thought it necessary. He suggested I take just one other person for moral support, since he didn't know yet where I was going. I opted for the Masculine One, since she was, after all, the toughest in the group.

"Walk through the French doors and out into the foyer," Dr. Townes instructed. "You will notice a corridor along the left side of the staircase, which is in the center of the foyer."

The others stood by the French doors, leaning into the glass panes to get a better view while Little Me, the Masculine One, and I walked closer to the corridor. "We're there, Doctor," I said.

"Now, walk down the corridor and tell me how many doors are on either side and at the end, and describe your surroundings as you walk." We obliged, clinging to each other's hands. It was dark again, like before, with only a couple of dim, yellow bulbs along the long narrow ceiling. Suddenly, the door slammed shut behind us. The door appeared very large, with no windows, and was made of solid wood with a peep hole drilled into it. Then it disappeared. As I turned back toward the end of the hallway, it began to look eerily familiar to me.

"Count the doors for me, would you please?" asked Dr. Townes.

I counted one, two, three, four, five doors on the right of the corridor, each with four panels and old chipping white paint covering the worn wood on them, which I described to the therapist. There were no doors on the left side of the corridor, only a solid wall, painted in a dark color that only intensified our shadows. A rather large ball of light from four evenly spaced light bulbs on the ceiling created illuminating spotlights in the otherwise dim hallway. As we walked down the corridor past the third door, half opened, I noticed a bathroom.

"This is Maw's damn house!" shouted the Masculine One. She said she hated Maw's house. I recognized Maw's weird toilet with the huge ceramic-like thing on the top, from which dangled a long, black chain and a dirty wooden pull handle that we used to flush the toilet. There was that cast iron and porcelain tub with the claw feet that I was afraid of being near because Maw's nasty cats hid under it and frightened me whenever I went into the bathroom.

"Okay," I said, trying to remain calm, and pressing hard on the Masculine One's hand, clenching my hand into a fist with hers. "Okay, I'm in Maw's house. Something terrible must have gone on in here, or I wouldn't be here."

Dr. Townes asked, "Who is Maw?"

Maw was my father's mother, I explained. She was my grandmother, but I never felt treated like a granddaughter. She was craggy like old weather-beaten wood, with a personality that snapped like crab claws at the slightest touch. She was short and skinny, with short straight hair, edges ragged from the damage she caused by burning it needlessly with a straightening comb all too often. She wore an apron all of the time, because she cooked and baked all the time. She had a long, bony nose and beady eyes. She walked bent over so that it looked like she had a hump in her back, even though she didn't. On her right index finger was a large semi-round lump of hard flesh that rose from her finger from the middle knuckle to the nail; "a tumor," she called it. She was a crotchety old thing, a real witch; the kind like in scary stories. As we continued down the hallway, the Masculine One was visibly agitated and held tightly to my grip on her hand.

Little Me seemed the most determined to continue. Townes was silent now; I supposed he was taking copious notes again. I asked, "Doctor, why must I be at Maw's house? I'm sure there aren't very many experiences I need to find out about here." He didn't answer.

"I'm getting nervous now," I said, biting the skin of my index finger; I had already chewed what nail was left.

The Masculine One let go of my hand and placed Little Me in back of her and then me in back of Little Me. "I am going to protect you both," she said.

While I certainly appreciated that the Masculine One wanted to help, I couldn't stop myself from shouting at her. "How the hell can you protect us in here? You're as vulnerable as we are."

Hearing what I said to the Masculine One, Dr. Townes instructed the three of us to move on and not to worry. "I want you to continue to explore," he said.

We continued on, past the bathroom to the old, dirty kitchen, where Maw used to bake and cook. I noticed the stove on the right near some painted wooden cabinets, and the table in the middle where she rolled and flattened the flour for biscuits. There was the sink directly in the back, and the window that opened to a brick wall on the other side. We moved past the kitchen and then past Uncle Ely's room, another hiding place for the many cats that lived with Maw. This time, though, there was no big black cat with the big black face and whiskers jumping out, hissing at me. Walking in single file, with the Masculine One in front, Little Me behind her and me behind Little Me, we finally reached the end of the corridor. On the slight right of the end of the corridor was one French door, which led to Maw's cluttered bedroom. On the left, two more French doors led to the large living room.

"We're at the end of the tour," I told the therapist. "I guess we can go back now."

"Who is in the kitchen?" he asked. Little Me moved from between us and walked back toward the kitchen.

"It's Maw! She's such a witch! I don't like her because she beat me if I fell asleep on the couch before dinner," Little Me said.

The Masculine One grew more agitated and said, "I remember that I wanted to punch her lights out so many times. She was so damn nasty to me because she said that I reminded her of Mom. That's why I burned up her favorite pink chiffon blouse in the bathroom and hid the ashes under Uncle Ely's bed."

They walked back to the kitchen opening and there Maw was, silently cooking, coughing, cooking, and smoking those wretched Pall Mall cigarettes so far down to the filter until there was nothing left but ashes and filter dangling from her lips. I could never figure out how she always managed to keep the ashes dangling on that filter, even when she spoke. There she was, coughing deep, the phlegm so thick in her throat that she choked a couple of times in mid cough. Somehow, those ashes wouldn't fall.

"Well," said the Masculine One, "unless she made rice or mashed potatoes. The ashes always made their way to my dinner plate."

While we reminisced about Maw's ashes, Little Me disappeared unexpectedly, which infuriated the Masculine One. Sparks and bits of orange glow were emanating from her body. She looked like she was going to burst back into that crimson fireball I met in the beginning of therapy.

"Doctor Townes, we have a problem! Little Me disappeared and the Masculine One is about to explode because of it. I'm afraid!" I exclaimed.

Townes spoke in his calm, fatherly voice, and the one that the Masculine One seemed to trust the most. "Calm down. Little Me is in the Living room. She has put herself into the apartment to help you remember."

"Goddammit!" shouted the Masculine One. "I have already remembered. I spent a great deal of time here, and it wasn't pleasant!" She managed to extinguish the red and yellow flames from her body, leaving only a small amount of smoke in its wake, but was still very agitated. "Does Little Me have to go through this shit again just so this one can remember?"

The therapist assured the Masculine One that Little Me would not be hurt, and that the process had to proceed for the benefit of all of us. Notwithstanding his assurances, however, consoling the Masculine One was useless, and I was fearful of what I would see, like in the other sessions. It was as though I had to travel all the way around the block just to get to the corner. Perhaps if I just kept telling myself that these experiences had to happen, I could get through them; that once I finally got to the corner, I'd be where I was supposed to be, and maybe even all the better for it.

Dr. Townes instructed us to go to the living room where we saw a slightly older Little Me playing by a huge picture window. She looked like she could be about six years old. It was daytime, and Little Me was playing by herself with about three little pretend dolls that she'd fashioned out of wooden clothes pins taken from Maw's clothes pin bag, lying beside her on the small covered stool where she sat. She seemed oblivious to us. I walked over to her to touch her and my hand swiped through her, as though she was made of mist.

"She's a figment. I understand now," I told the Masculine One, who was silently standing attention, almost militaristic, and watching my every move, protecting me, I was sure.

After a time, two boys came running into the room. They were playing together, one chasing the other, until one of them spotted Little Me over by the window. I watched intently as Little Me ignored the noise and commotion that the boys were making.

I squinted to get a better look at the two boys. I walked over to the smaller boy and looked into his face, dead on. It was my brother, Edward, but not grown up, only about seven years old. I watched as my brother tried to divert the attention of the larger boy away from Little Me, punching and running, getting caught, and then getting away, repeating the scenario over and over. I took a walk over to the larger boy. He was my cousin, Bobby. I instantly felt the tiny hairs on my back stand on end. Bobby was trying to move toward Little Me and my brother was trying to keep him away.

Bobby leaned into Edward's face and whispered, "I got a big box from Maw's washin' machine in the back room. Let's go get it and trap the cats in it." They snickered to themselves and appeared delighted at the prospect of trapping the cats. They left the living room in a rush to grab the hefty washing machine box, racing each other down the corridor until they disappeared.

"Can we go back to the Safe Room, now?" I nervously asked my therapist. "I got a chance to see my cousin and my brother from back then. I can pretty much figure out that I didn't have fun here."

Townes did not reply. The Masculine One got in front of me as if guarding me from the boys who had reentered the living room, dragging the huge washing machine box. As they struggled to get the box into the living room, Bobby stared at Little Me and snickered to himself. Inside the box were about a dozen assorted cats, including the huge black cat with the long whiskers that I remembered from long ago. There were gray cats, calico cats, tabby cats, white cats, and brown spotted cats. They were all scratching each other, hissing and yelping. Some of them were tied up but others were piled on top of each other, none seemingly able to escape from the washing machine box. Edward was laughing loudly and pushing many of the peeking cat heads back into the bottom of the box. When they got the box into the living room, Little Me looked up at them with a start.

"Run! Run! Get the hell out of there!" yelled the Masculine One, pleading with Little Me. As though she heard the Masculine One, Little Me got up from where she was sitting near the large picture window and tried to run toward the corridor to the kitchen where Maw was cooking and choking. Bobby chased Little Me, catching her by the hem of her dress and trapping her. He grabbed her around the waist and threw her onto the couch, holding her down with the weight of his body.

"Come over here and hold her legs!" Bobby commanded Edward, who obliged willingly, laughing as Bobby tied Little Me by the feet and legs with rope he found in Maw's clothes pin bag.

After they finished tying Little Me, Bobby and Edward stood over her, laughing and taunting, "Cry baby, cry!" Little Me was screaming and crying, kicking and thrashing, flailing in an attempt to get away from them.

The Masculine One placed her arm around my shoulders and pulled me to her for comfort, but it was no use. Overcome with sadness and helplessness, I began to sob. I simply couldn't believe that Maw was right in the next room, right in the kitchen. What was she doing that she couldn't hear what was going on in the living room? Why wasn't she coming to rescue Little Me from Bobby and Edward? Questions raced through my head. "I want to leave this place, Doctor Townes," I pleaded, "Please, don't make me stay in here. Please let me leave!"

The therapist still did not respond.

I closed my eyes so I didn't have to watch, but strangely, I could still see through my lids. I saw Bobby pushing his pimple-filled, greasy face into hers, at the forehead, pressing in closely, yelling and spitting into her face.

"We're gonna fix you!" He commanded Edward to grab Little Me by the legs. He took hold of one leg, then the other. Little Me tried desperately to kick him but wasn't able to because of her restraints. When Edward finally had both legs, Bobby took hold of her arms, and together, they swung her violently, back and forth, like a hammock tied between two trees in a windstorm.

They sang, "Heave ho!" and counted gleefully together as they swung, "One, two, three!" and then heaved Little Me into the box with the cats they had captured earlier. Obviously proud of what they had done, each grabbed the other's hand, raised their arms together into the air once and shook hands when they lowered their arms.

I couldn't see or hear Little Me anymore, only rustling in the box. I ran over to the box and peered inside to see if she was there, and to my surprise, she and the cats had disappeared.

"Show's over," the Masculine One said. She appeared tired and ready to shed the entire experience. "Let's go back."

We walked through the corridor to the kitchen. "Stop," I said to the Masculine One. "There's Little Me."

Little Me was in the kitchen. Her face, arms, and legs were scratched. Her pretty dress was torn and dirty, stained with cat urine, and she was smelly.

Her hair was a mess. She was trying to get Maw's attention and Maw was ignoring her, as she usually did. For a brief moment, I wondered whether Maw could even see her.

Answer her!" I yelled to Maw, but I knew that Maw couldn't hear me. "Look at her, you old witch! Don't you see she's hurt?" I could see Maw deliberately ignoring her. Each time Maw stopped, Little Me tried to gain her attention, but Maw would step away, walking in another direction. "What a bitch!" the Masculine One chimed in.

We were mortified, both of us, as we watched helplessly while Little Me tried to get help from Maw. Finally, Maw turned around to Little Me, and bent down to face her, the smoke from her cigarette choking Little Me into a fit of coughing. "Aww, them boys ain't hurtin' eeeyuu!" she barked between the coughing and choking, with her slow, Midwestern drawl.

Little Me ran out of the kitchen, past us, through the hall and to the door of the Safe Room. The Masculine One and I rushed quickly to get to the door, fearing that it would disappear again.

Jesus was standing near the fireplace when we returned to the Safe Room. Dr. Townes recited his customary prayer as one by one, all returned to Jesus, watched carefully by the four angels who were on guard at the four corners of the room, until Jesus disappeared into me. I returned to the therapist's office, exhausted, but strangely at ease.

When I walked out to the parking lot to retrieve my car for the long ride home, I noticed that the sky was a wash of deep dark grays and navy blues. I sat in the car with the key in the ignition, though I hadn't yet started it. I sat motionless for a while to collect my thoughts and the thoughts of all the others who wanted in on the commotion inside my head.

"Order, *order*!" yelled the Perfectionist. "We have to handle this with order and composure."

I agreed. "Everyone can't talk at the same time and be understood," I said. We all agreed that Maw was detestable. Then the Masculine One sighed a long, deliberate sigh of relief, started the ignition, and drove us home.

Week Twenty-Two

The Masculine One was unsettled all week. Going back to Maw's house had been extremely stressful for her, which made each day at work rather disconcerting for me. Although the Perfectionist tried hard to help me keep composed during the day, the Masculine One twisted and turned in my head, churning and burning like acid reflux in my throat. Big Fat overindulged in her favorite white chocolate truffles all week, which caused diarrhea for three days. The Chatterbox droned on incessantly about life at Maw's and just about everything else. Of course she had good reason, she said, reminding me that it was for my own benefit. I was convinced I had gone completely insane.

The Chatterbox took me through flashbacks again, showing my visits to Maws. She explained that my visits started when I was four, about the time when my mother separated from my father and moved to Philadelphia from New York City. Daddy would arrive in Philadelphia right before Christmas Day to fetch us from Nana's house, where we lived, and drive the long cold drive into the Bronx because he sometimes had no heat in his car. He also came to pick us up when school let out for the summer; his car hot and steaming because it had no air conditioning. He always stopped the car on East 169th Street and Boston Road, where I could remember a clean, black and white tiled building on one corner, tenements on both corners across the street, and a large building on the fourth corner, where Maw lived on the first floor. My mother told me that we lived there together with Daddy for a time, but I must have been too young to remember.

The Chatterbox explained how it was always dark outside by the time we got to Maw's. Daddy would walk us into the apartment, kiss us, and then send us away so he could chat with Maw, and maybe smoke a cigarette with her before he left us for the entire Christmas holiday or the whole summer. He would put on his camel colored overcoat and matching Fedora and then head for the door. When the door closed, I would run to the huge picture window in the living room to catch a glimpse of Daddy leaving. I would bang on the window glass and wave, hoping he would look up and see me, but he would never look up. He would get into his car and drive off into the distance. I recalled how I would sit at the window for as long as I could to watch his car disappear down 169th Street, and how night after night, I would look out of the huge picture window into the dark, hoping he would return soon.

I would sit there in my self-induced hypnotic trance until interrupted by a push or a pull off the stool that I sat on near the window. When it was my brother wanting to play, he would get my attention for a while. Sometimes, though, it was Bobby with an open-handed smack in the head, his trademark greeting for me and my brother.

As I listened to The Chatterbox, images of Bobby flashed. I recalled him being older than we were by about five years. He was the third oldest of a bunch of kids from my daddy's sister, Gladys. Bobby had piercing gray-blue eyes and kept his hair cut very close to his scalp. He had a large scar in the middle of his forehead that looked like someone had once landed a hatchet there.

The Masculine One chimed into the flashback, saying how Bobby liked to play too much. "Tricks," she called them, and mostly on Little Me, but sometimes on my brother if he didn't cooperate. The Chatterbox then explained how his tricks were always mean spirited and cruel.

"One day, for instance," said the Masculine One, "while making Maw's bed, he stopped Little Me and said, 'Hey, let's play a game.' I knew his games usually ended badly, but Little Me was gullible. He made her hop around until her free foot landed into a pile of cat poop he'd placed near her feet while her eyes were closed."

The Chatterbox joined back in. "He laughed hysterically, coaxing our brother into laughter as well. They ended up getting Little Me beat because Maw thought she was playing instead of making the bed, and because she tracked the cat poop into the kitchen when she ran in there to tell Maw what Bobby had done."

The Chatterbox recounted another occasion when Little Me was playing by herself out in the hallway, swinging on the huge door that separated the vestibule from the common foyer in the apartment building. Bobby pulled Little Me off the door in mid-swing, and commanded my brother to hold her against the wall. She wrestled to try to escape, but the two of them held her too tightly.

The Masculine One interrupted, "Then that bastard pulled a dead chicken head from his pocket, worked his index and middle fingers through its neck and managed to make the chicken's mouth move up and down. He pushed the chicken head into her face, taunting and pecking her with its beak, while they both laughed heartily and chanted, 'Cocka Doodle Do! Cocka Doodle Do! Cocka Doodle Do!'"

It was getting late and I wanted to get some sleep, but again, as had become customary for her, The Chatterbox remained relentless in her yammering. Worse still, the Masculine One was just as talkative, mainly because she was there through all of it. The Masculine One talked about how Bobby liked to torture the cats that Maw kept in the house, and how he trapped them, tied them up, and lit matches under them. He didn't kill them, though, opting for the torture instead.

I also remembered how he mistreated Maw's cats, and I figured that he probably got more thrills from the terror in their eyes and their yelps and screams than he could get from ending their lives, until two of the cats disappeared. Maw thought they had somehow gotten out of the apartment and were just lost. Besides, Maw would never suspect Bobby; she thought that Bobby never did anything bad. The Chatterbox said that Maw thought I made things up about Bobby. Both the Masculine One and The Chatterbox agreed that Bobby had probably set those cats on fire in the ally of the apartment building one afternoon. I thought so, too, but was always just too afraid to go back there to see, and too afraid to ask, for fear that he might decide to do the same thing to me.

It was 3:00 a.m. and I pleaded with the two of them to let me sleep. Reluctantly, they finally obliged. I kissed my husband, covered my head with the bedspread, and went to sleep.

Week Twenty-Three

The persistent chatter about Maw and Bobby was overwhelming and made me feel uneasy enough to discuss it with Dr. Townes in the Safe Room. *Just to make sure nothing else happened to me that I might have repressed,* I thought.

"Who is in the room with you today?" the therapist asked.

I explained that it was quiet, with only the Masculine One and Little Me in the room, perhaps because of more issues concerning Maw's house.

He asked us to go back through the door we had been through when we first saw Maw's house. This time it was dark outside. Little Me disappeared once again as we walked slowly down the dimly lit hallway toward the French doors at the end.

The Masculine One whispered, "Bedtime at Maw's was repulsive." When we got to Maw's bedroom, I immediately saw what she meant. There in her bed were my brother, Bobby, and Little Me.

"With all the bedrooms in that house, why would she put Little Me in the bed with two boys?" I asked.

Dr. Townes didn't respond, but I didn't expect him to anyway. I was there to observe. The people in the bed were figments, there to help me remember repressed memories.

As was the case every night, Maw passed me and kissed Bobby and my brother good night, turned off the lamp by the bed, and then walked out into the dark, leaving Little Me alone with them. After a while, I heard Bobby whisper into the air, "Cocka Doodle Do!" and watched as his thick, clammy fingers crawled up her legs to touch Little Me in her private parts. I tried to close my eyes but again saw directly through my lids.

The Masculine One drew me close to her and hugged my shoulders as I cried softly to myself, distraught over the terror Little Me was feeling, and over my own inability to intervene. I stood helplessly by as Little Me screeched in pain when Bobby dug too deeply and scratched her inside with his dirty fingernails. The noise woke my brother, who sat up, watching Bobby while he made a game out of how many fingers he could put into her vagina at one time.

The Masculine One tensed up and whispered, "When he played this game, I wanted to kill him, but Little Me wouldn't bring me up." The Masculine One wiped away a small tear from her eye. We continued watching as Edward muffled her mouth to keep Little Me quiet, while she screamed in agony.

Suddenly, images of Bobby climbing on top of Little Me, and then rubbing his dry, scratchy penis on her private parts until she was sticky rushed to the surface and flooded my mind. Every single night, when she heard Bobby's whisper, she knew that it meant he was going to violate her again.

We were drawn back into the Safe Room where we found Little Me smiling and dancing around the room. She seemed oblivious to anything that happened through the door we had just come out of.

I explained to the therapist that there might have been another flashback during the time we were at Maws.

"What did you see?" he asked.

I told him about the last night of my summer at Maw's house when Bobby whispered, "Cocka Doodle Do!" and when he ran his index finger up to Little Me's private parts again, that the Masculine One threatened to kill him, and grabbed his hand, twisting his finger until it cracked. The Masculine One said she felt somewhat vindicated for other times when she couldn't help. Of course Bobby's finger didn't get broken that night, and I was confident that it was the Masculine One who'd saved the day again.

Before I left, Dr. Townes asked me to buy two books that I could use to journal. He said it would be part of my therapy now. One book would be for anything The Chatterbox wanted to tell me during times when I wasn't in therapy, and the other book was for Little Me to write down her thoughts. He said that each week he would collect and read them, then provide me with notes and feedback.

Chapter Thirteen

Week Twenty-six

After a long and boring day at work, I really wasn't in any mood for therapy, but I dragged myself anyway, after an inordinate amount of coaxing by The Chatterbox, who wanted to know what the therapist thought of her journal entries. By now, I was weary of all the memories and rehashes, and she was by far the only one it seemed even remotely interested in discussing the past.

Along the route the trees were barren and brown, with only mud on the ground where an earlier snow had melted. It was bitterly cold, and the wind tapped hard against my cheek as I left the car for my appointment. I walked into the waiting room and noticed I had forgotten the journal.

Oh well, I thought, *it's much too cold. I'm not going back to the car.*

"*Oh yes you are*!" shouted The Chatterbox, numbing my inner ear. Dr. Townes was in the hallway that separated his office from the waiting room. I smiled nervously as I told him that The Chatterbox wasn't going to let me leave the journal in the car, and then went out to retrieve it.

"Make yourself comfortable," he began. He took the journal and placed it among some other books and papers he had on his desk. "I'll read it and return it next week." The Chatterbox was disappointed when he said that he needed time to read the journal. She expected that he would read and discuss it at the same time.

"That's fine," I said, even though I knew it wasn't fine with The Chatterbox.

When I arrived in the Safe Room, it felt inviting, warm and toasty, made so by the crackling fire in the fireplace. The sky was really pretty outside the large bow window, not at all the way it looked on the way to the therapist's office. There was a great deal of fresh, powdery snow outside.

Must have been a storm, I thought. The large tree to the left of center in the beautiful garden was bare, and the only thing left of the flowers were the stems, most of which were hidden by snowdrifts, but it was beautiful, clean, and white. The Perfectionist admired the powdery snow banks and talked about how happy she was that nothing had walked across them to disturb them. Little Me was looking out of the large bow window at the right, using the frost on the window glass to practice her name in cursive. The others were all assembled and seated on the couch. They all sat stoically, except for The Chatterbox, who paced back and forth, from the French doors to the fireplace and back again, back and forth, apparently irritated by having to wait until all were in the room before she could begin.

Dr. Townes instructed me to go through the French doors to the foyer and stand at the large round table. He said, "I want Little Me to choose someone to join you."

Little Me entered the foyer with Sick and Tired, apparently shocked at being chosen. "Why me?" she asked. "I can't possibly have anything to contribute. Besides, I am not quite the same, since we got on the meds," she said, reluctant to join me and Little Me and hoping to be excused from the session's exercise.

"Little Me, who did you choose to accompany you?" Townes asked.

"I chose Sick and Tired," Little Me said. She took Sick and Tired by the hand and squeezed it, which managed to elicit a tiny smile from Sick and Tired's cracked, chapped lips.

"Well, then, that's good," Dr. Townes said approvingly. He directed us to walk up the staircase ahead of us. "I'd like you to go up the stairs to the top of the landing."

We walked, all three, side by side up the wide staircase made of white marble instead of the wood it had been before, until we got to the top of the landing.

Directly ahead were three tall doors, very ornately decorated, fancy and beautiful.

"What do you see?" he asked.

"Three really fancy doors, and the floor is white marble. It's all very pretty," I said. The others nodded in agreement.

"Then choose one of the doors and walk through it," said the therapist.

Both Sick and Tired and I were apprehensive about choosing between one of the three doors, pretty or not, since our experience exploring the Victorian house had brought about a great deal of anguish. Sensing our uneasiness, Little Me ran toward the center door and flung it open for us.

The door opened and suddenly we were standing in the small front yard of a home that looked like an English Tudor manor. Tall fir trees stood on either side of the front door. Little Me ran up to the arched entryway and opened the door. We entered into an enormous living room with a fireplace in the corner. Large dark wooden beams appeared to float across a high, vaulted ceiling. A lengthy staircase along the wall, with a beautiful wrought iron railing that extended its length, curled where the steps turned. The railing met and was joined by a large wrought iron post at the foot of the steps. Medieval lantern-like sconces with light bulbs that resembled flickering candlesticks flanked the fireplace, beside which a wrought iron gate, tools, and a firewood storage container stood. Although somewhat dated, the expensive furniture throughout the living room was tastefully appointed. Straight ahead were three wide steps that spanned the width of the living room and led to the formal dining room. The house felt familiar. I'd been there before.

Apparently anticipating my thoughts, Little Me smiled and said, "Yes. This is Aunt Elise's house." I always loved Aunt Elise's house. Hers was the one by which all other houses I would ever see and want to live in were measured.

I thought about The Chatterbox back in the Safe Room. She had written about Aunt Elise's house and wanted to talk about it, but Little Me hadn't chosen her to come with us. She would certainly be stewing right now if she knew we were here.

We continued to explore, walking through the kitchen, where we noticed chicken frying in a pan on the stove. In the finished basement, we noted yet another huge fireplace and many, many toys. We left the basement and started up the winding staircase to the bedrooms, where we saw Aunt Elise and Uncle Harry's room, my cousin Joanie's room, and my cousin Baby Justin's nursery.

On the way back down the stairs, we heard people talking. They were sitting at the dining room table, eating fried chicken and drinking liquor. To my surprise, it was Aunt Elise, Uncle Harry, and a celebrity that they were entertaining. Celebrities always frequented my Aunt Elise's house. Uncle Harry was a famous record producer. Seeing them had a bittersweet tinge to it because I loved them both very dearly, but both Aunt Elise, Uncle Harry, and all their children were long dead now from drugs, alcohol, or disease.

My session ended for the day, and I was thankful that there was no upheaval of repressed or blocked memories. I returned to the therapist's office, where he promised The Chatterbox an audience at the next session.

Week Twenty-seven

The Chatterbox was excited all week in anticipation of being center stage at the therapy session. She intended to do all of the talking and was all aflutter in my head the entire day at work. She wanted to discuss what she'd written in the journals and was thrilled to have yet another medium in which to express herself.

"The mighty pen" she boasted. "I am the queen of words! That's why I do the writing for everybody! It's because I command the English language. I own it! I know how to put words together and I'm not afraid of public speaking, either. Just put me in front of a bunch of people and I shine! I'm a brilliant orator!"

Her supercilious enthusiasm annoyed me and reverberated through my head all the way to Dr. Townes' office. I pulled into the parking lot and found a space well away from the other cars. "Remember, no dings," whispered the Perfectionist.

Okay, I get it, I thought. *Another epiphany. You're the one who is just as concerned about dings in my car as my husband.*

As I entered the Safe Room, I was greeted by The Chatterbox, who was already there with Little Me. Then, one by one, each of the others arrived, until all were assembled. I was surprised and quite puzzled that the Masculine One had arrived quietly, and not through a blaze of fire and smoke. *Perhaps the meds are working on her, too*, I thought.

Dr. Townes asked Little Me if everybody was in the room, and she nodded. I chuckled because when Little Me nodded, the therapist wouldn't know she answered unless she answered through my mouth. I told him everyone was assembled. I laughed when I informed him that The Chatterbox was about to burst at the seams with excitement.

"Little Me," Dr. Townes began, "take The Chatterbox by the hand and walk her to the door on the left side of the large bow window."

A small door, smaller in scale than the size of the room, appeared. Little Me took The Chatterbox's hand and then The Chatterbox held my hand tightly, pulling me along, as Little Me opened the door and walked through. There we were, the three of us, standing in front of Aunt Elise's house, as it was, just as I remembered it.

The Chatterbox started talking immediately.

"Daddy would take Little Me to Aunt Elise's house, and my brother to Aunt Gladys' house sometimes, when Maw didn't want to be bothered with either of them, at least not for an entire summer."

The Chatterbox let go of my hand. She walked ahead of Little Me and let go of her hand as well. At the arched front door she peered through the wrought-iron-clad window. "There's Aunt Elise, in the dining room! She looks so beautiful."

The Chatterbox opened the door and entered the huge sunken living room. I followed and sat on Aunt Elise's stunning contemporary sectional.

I looked around for Little Me, but she'd disappeared, as she did so often when something dreadfully wrong was about to happen.

Dr. Townes reminded us, "You are not participants in here. You are simply viewing." He reassured us that Little Me would not be hurt. "Remember that once Little Me enters the room, she is simply a figment of your recollection, and she is not reliving or even feeling the experiences."

The Chatterbox and I watched as Aunt Elise fried chicken in the kitchen and prepared the dining room for entertaining. A cigarette in a decorative ashtray on the dining room table smoldered, its ashes trailing the length of the ashtray where it had burned, indicating she had not smoked it since it was lit. The house was full of great smells: food, flowers, and Aunt Elise's Chanel perfume.

I thought of how wonderfully they lived. Aunt Elise was rich, and her house oozed opulence. Celebrities were always visiting Aunt Elise and Uncle Harry, who were always entertaining whenever I visited. They lived much better than Aunt Gladys, who lived in the projects in Brooklyn, or Maw, who lived in a rundown tenement in the Bronx. Uncle Harry was a famous songwriter and producer and had made a beautiful home for his family on Long Island.

The Chatterbox was uncharacteristically quiet as she rose from the couch and walked to the beautiful wrought iron railing on the stairs, motioning for me to join her. We walked up the long winding stairs to the top of the landing, where I heard the sound of children playing in one of the rooms. We peeked inside and there was Little Me, playing alone with a great dollhouse. The huge house was made of wood, with a tall gable roof and many rooms. The front of the house looked like the front of Aunt Elise's house, and the dollhouse rooms were decorated in the same style.

The Chatterbox entered the room and began to describe its surroundings for Dr. Townes. "This room is so beautiful! And so pink! A perfect little girl's room."

"Where are you?" he asked.

"In Joanie's room," said The Chatterbox.

"Her bedroom looks just like what I always wanted my bedroom to look like," I said.

"Is Joanie there?" he asked. We looked around, but Joanie was not in the room. The Chatterbox told us that the dollhouse was custom built by the same people who had built Aunt Elise's house. I wasn't surprised. They were rich, and as I recalled, Joanie was a spoiled little rich girl.

I could tell how much Little Me loved playing with the dollhouse. I'd always wanted to have something like that myself. We continued to watch as she walked two little dolls up the stairs of the dollhouse and placed them into different, beautifully decorated rooms. She took a small baby carriage and placed it by the front door. Then she placed two more dolls into chairs in the dining room and began speaking for them in much the same way that Aunt Elise and Uncle Harry did many times in their dining room. We continued to watch

Little Me play quietly by herself in the bedroom, singing and talking for the dolls. After a while, a little girl, her large ponytail swinging wildly back and forth stormed into the room.

"Why are you playing with my dollhouse? Did I give you permission?" Joanie snatched the two dolls that Little Me had in her hands and threw them to the other side of the bedroom where they landed on her white rocking chair by the window. She pushed past Little Me to the dollhouse, kicking her slightly as she shoved the dollhouse back to the area where it rested when not in play.

The Chatterbox shouted, "That little budding bitch! She *never* played with that dollhouse."

"I'll help you put it back," Little Me said.

"No! I told you, don't touch my toys unless I give you permission. I did NOT give you permission!" Joanie shouted while she struggled to move the huge, heavy dollhouse. Little Me quietly got off the floor and left the pretty pink bedroom. We followed as she headed for the stairs.

Downstairs, four little girls, all about eight, nine or possibly ten years old were seated around a chair that had been placed in the middle of the floor. Little Me looked older; The Chatterbox confirmed she was about eight.

"That would make would make Joanie about eleven," I said.

The Chatterbox was becoming visibly agitated, pacing the floor around the four little girls in the room. "This is where Joanie played really stupid games with Little Me," said The Chatterbox. "Sick and Tired told me that she came out a lot at Aunt Elise's house."

I was shocked. I only remembered fun times at Aunt Elise's house and couldn't imagine why Sick and Tired would emerge here at all.

"Sick and Tired told me that Joanie was a spoiled brat, and she was jealous of Little Me." The Chatterbox continued pacing around the children seated in the room. "She was jealous if her family and friends paid attention to anybody but her. I always tried to tell Aunt Elise, but Aunt Elise wouldn't punish her."

The children were indeed playing a game, and of course, Joanie was in command of it. "You're going to be part of our club, but you have to go through our initiation to get in," she said as she reminded the participants that Little Me wanted to be a member of their exclusive club.

The Chatterbox leaned in closely to me and whispered into my ear. "That word is too big for Little Me to understand!" She lamented for a moment over not lending Little Me a helping hand back then. "I should have come out then, but there was no reason for me to believe I had to step in for her, and she didn't ask me."

I searched Little Me's face, and could see that she was confused.

"What's an initiation? What do I have to do?" asked Little Me.

"Nothing yet" Joanie said arrogantly, waiving her hands and popping her neck from side to side. "We are going to blindfold you, and then you will have to figure out what things are when we tell you to, without peeking."

"Uh, okay." Little Me shrugged as The Chatterbox and I watched intently.

"I know *exactly* what she is going to do!" The Chatterbox whispered into my ear.

"I remember, too. Let me watch for myself." I whispered back, even though I really didn't remember much.

Joanie blindfolded Little Me tightly and placed a knot in the back of the tie. She then snapped her finger and motioned for one of the girls to "get the stuff." The children raised Little Me to her feet and walked her to the chair, which was placed in the middle of the living room floor for her. Then they sat her down with a push and a thud.

One of the children placed a strawberry in front of Little Me, waving it close to her nose, and then rubbing it gently around her lips. Little Me licked her lips and tasted the juicy strawberry juice. "Ummmm. That's a strawberry." Everyone clapped with approval at the correct answer. Little Me raised her shoulders slightly, as if satisfied that she did well, and confident that she would continue to do so.

Appearing not as approving as the others, Joanie said, "That one was easy."

Another little girl took a feather from the pile of stuff and walked over to Little Me. She waved the feather around the top of her forehead and drew an outline of her face with the tip, slightly touching her face, just enough so that it tickled. She shoved the feather tip partly up one of Little Me's nostrils, causing her to sneeze.

Rubbing her nose and laughing a bit from the tickle, Little Me said, "That has got to be a feather." The children laughed gleefully and clapped, and Little Me smiled.

Two down, I thought, wondering how many more tests she would have to take.

Joanie was getting visibly disturbed by the small successes Little Me was enjoying. "Those things are too easy. You need to pick something hard," she admonished the girls.

Another little girl walked over to the pile of things and found a jar of mayonnaise. She opened the jar and placed it in front of Little Me, the lid side toward her face.

"What is this?" she asked. Little Me felt around but could not feel anything, since the jar was a bit too far for her to reach. "I thought that you were going to put things on me for me to guess," Little Me said, sensing she might be disqualified by this next test.

The little girl held the mayonnaise jar closer to Little Me. "What do I do?" asked Little Me, fidgeting a bit in the chair. Joanie snatched the jar of mayonnaise out of the little girl's hand, spilling a small portion on the floor. Then Joanie motioned for the little girl to sit back down, dismissing her as a failure. Standing in the middle of the room, Joanie snapped her finger and announced, "I'm changing the initiation. You will have to guess stuff by following MY directions." Joanie closed the jar of mayonnaise and stood motionless for a moment.

"I know *exactly* what that bitch in waiting is getting ready to do!" said The Chatterbox. "Sick and Tired said that she—"

I cut her off and admonished The Chatterbox for trying to tell me.

Joanie's baby brother, Justin, was toddling up the stairs to the dining room, his diaper soiled. Joanie ran ahead of him to the kitchen and retrieved a large cooking spoon from the drawer, then returned and scooped some of Baby Justin's feces with it. She walked directly in front of Little Me and commanded, "Stick your finger right here."

Little Me put her finger into the air.

"Point it straight ahead!" Joanie said as she aimed the spoon of wet poop at Little Me's finger. "Move your finger left, move it LEFT!" Joanie shouted as her friends sat stunned.

Little Me moved her finger left. "Move your finger right." Little Me moved her finger slightly to the right. "MOVE IT MORE TO THE RIGHT! MOVE IT RIGHT!" Joanie screamed. "Now poke your finger RIGHT IN HERE!" Little Me plunged her finger into the wet, gooey dung.

"Ugh! What is this?" Little Me asked, then placed her finger to her nose. "It's doodoo, you doodoo girl! You put your fingers into doodoo! Doodoo girl! Doodoo girl!" Joanie shouted and chanted.

The other girls looked at each other, then at Joanie, and began to chant, "Doodoo girl! Doodoo girl!"

Joanie pulled the spoon away from Little Me and began to dance around the chair, singing and chanting, "Doodoo girl!"

Little Me just sat in that chair while the other girls chanted and sang, calling her Doodoo girl. I was so embarrassed for her, so sad that my cousin Joanie was cruel to her, and had enticed her friends to be cruel as well.

Little Me sat in the chair, not moving, holding out her finger while the poop dripped to the floor. Joanie reached over the back of the chair and yanked at the blindfold, jerking Little Me to the back of the chair. It was untied and thrown over her head, revealing that Little Me was crying.

Joanie yelled, "You couldn't guess what it was, so you aren't in my club."

Mortified, Little Me looked at the mess on her finger and rushed upstairs to wash her hands.

Joanie yelled up stairs, "And you better not tell my mother, or I'll beat you up!"

Recollections raced through my mind. I asked The Chatterbox, "When did Sick and Tired emerge here? Was it when I couldn't remember?"

The Chatterbox wasn't talking; instead, she was concentrating on Little Me. She followed Little Me up the stairs while I picked up the rear. When we both got to the landing at the top of the stairs, we noticed that Little Me was in Aunt Elise and Uncle Harry's room, at the window, talking to herself. We walked into the room and approached the window so we could hear her.

"I wish I could die. I want to climb out of this window and kill myself," she whispered. She climbed onto the window ledge from the chair where she was sitting and unlatched the window lock. Then she struggled to open the window, which had no screen. She reached out of the window with her tiny little arms and was at once out of the window and on her knees on the ledge outside. My heart fell into my stomach, and I could feel the burning in my chest. Was Little Me actually trying to kill herself? *Not at that young age, that's impossible! Just preposterous!* I thought.

Joanie was in the room now, at the window screaming, "Get back in here before you fall!" She grabbed Little Me with both arms around her waist and dragged her back through the window into the room. At that moment, I could feel the pain behind the look in Little Me's eyes. It was undeniably true that Sick and Tired had emerged and was outside on that window ledge with her that day.

When I returned to the therapist's office from the Safe Room, I remembered in vivid detail what happened to Little Me. I felt extremely sad and began to recall other episodes of cruelty at the hands of my spoiled, rich cousin. The Chatterbox wanted to spill much more about life at Aunt Elise's, but my time for the session had ended.

"I'm increasing your Zoloft to one hundred fifty milligrams," Dr. Townes said, writing another prescription.

On the ride home, my attempts to elicit conversation only extracted a few sighs and some dry yawns. I decided that it was too futile to get a conversation going with any of them. *All right, so much for that,* I thought. It was evident they were all miffed that I took that prescription from the therapist. *I'm being ostracized by them,* I thought. *Good, then. So be it. Maybe I'll get a good night's sleep.*

When I finally got home, I took my pills, went straight to bed, and foolishly anticipated a good night's sleep.

Chapter Fourteen

"Wake up." A voice disturbed my sleep. My eyes opened wide. The clock read 4:06 in the morning. "Wake up," the voice repeated. It was Sick and Tired.

"I need to tell you something. I'm feeling like I won't be part of us anymore. Maybe it's the medication. Somehow I don't feel like I'm needed anymore."

I sat up, grabbed the bottle of sparkling water that I kept on my night table, and took a sip.

"I'm not feeling like I can help matters much anymore." She winced.

I plumped my pillow, and placed it onto the back of my headboard, closed my eyes, and rested my head. "Listen," I said, "you're an important part of my overall therapy. Just hang in there. The medication is making you feel this way." Sick and Tired didn't respond, and I tried to go back to sleep.

"Wake up." Sick and Tired woke me again.

"What the hell?" I yelled, startling my husband, who was soundly asleep. I was angry now. I strained my eyes to look at the clock on the wall. It was 5:00 in the morning, and I had to get up at 6:30 for work. *Was she out of her mind?* I thought.

"You have got to stop taking the medication. It's killing me. I don't want to die, not just now."

I pleaded with Sick and Tired to stop. "Can we at least wait to discuss this at our next session?" I asked her. It was evident that there was no use in sleeping anymore, so I stayed awake until the clock read 6:30 and then got up for work. Then, for an entire week, at the same time each morning, Sick and Tired chose to whine. I tried ignoring her but found out quickly that it was easier for them to ignore me than for me to ignore them, since, of course, they were inside *my* head. Again and again I stayed awake, wide-eyed and angry, night after night, until 6:30 in the morning.

Week Twenty-Eight

The medication was definitely taking its toll on Sick and Tired. For that matter, I hadn't been hearing much from the Masculine One either, and certainly the day before, it seemed that they were all medicated into acquiescence. I was growing more and more ambivalent about taking the medication myself. The increased dosage appeared to have had quite different effects on the others, many showing the effects at the most inopportune times and places. Although only my dearest friends dared share their feelings with me, I knew my behavior was unusually erratic at work most times. For certain, my husband and family members noticed my changes in behavior at home. My days were spent alternating between being actively engaged in the ravings of the Masculine One, overeating with Big Fat, and sulking in misery courtesy of Sick and Tired. Other times, there was only complete silence and no engagement with the others at all. Usually, the Masculine One and the Perfectionist controlled the day's work, alternating tasks depending on the situations. Sick and Tired slept all day, which annoyed me, and then worked my nerves at night, brooding whenever I tried to sleep. The Chatterbox was conspicuous by her silence, and the Trollop lurked just inside, under the surface, not immediately obvious, but not completely unanticipated.

Today, their eerie silence continued during my drive to the therapist's office. There were only sighs and yawns coming out of my mouth; uncontrollable, it seemed, even though I was far from bored. My mind was blank, naught, not even my own thoughts. I was utterly numb.

While I sat in Dr. Townes' waiting room, Big Fat whispered, "You need one of those mints over there," referring to the peppermints in a bowl on the baker's rack shelf. I obliged her without protest, finding it increasingly difficult to deny Big Fat's requests for goodies. At about 4:35, Dr. Townes walked in.

The Perfectionist emerged suddenly and checked my watch, miffed because he wasn't on time. "When you're late, you are on my time," she snipped through my mouth. Embarrassed, I apologized.

Once I was seated and comfortable in the therapist's office, I grew introspective, quite unexpectedly, and effectively blocked out the small banter going on between the others and Dr. Townes.

My thoughts were consumed with questions I knew I couldn't possibly answer myself. *The 'me' that I am today, wearing what I am wearing today, who is 'she?' When I'm not busy being engaged with one of the others, exactly who am I?* I wondered. *Who the hell am I? When I wake each morning, I dress to suit someone, whether it is the Masculine One, with her pressed suits and oxford shirts, or the Perfectionist, with her wonderful taste in the feminine. When Sick and Tired is close, I might remain unwashed and funky for days at a time.*

No one offered an explanation, not even The Chatterbox, who prided herself at knowing everything about everybody, and not afraid to tell it. Suddenly I felt like I had lost a thousand points in the game, as though I had thrown the dice and had to go back to the beginning of the board.

Dr. Townes had been talking to me for about fifteen minutes, but I was too deeply ensconced to hear him until he touched my shoulder. "What's wrong?" he asked.

I looked up at him, shrugging. "I think I had a relapse, Doctor. I think it's the medication. I don't know who I am anymore. I'm feeling especially disheartened that I haven't discovered myself through the others with me, and I am questioning who I am." As I spoke to him, I became increasingly more upset, and feared that perhaps through my sadness, Sick and Tired might take over. I immediately tried shaking off the feeling, so she wouldn't move to the front.

Dr. Townes wanted to reassure me. "I want you to understand something. Yes, the medication is working on those parts of the brain and all of you may be feeling somewhat strange as a result. But trust me, you are making tremendous progress. We are opening up those repressed areas and releasing the blocks that caused Little Me to fragment."

I could not argue with his assessment. I learned that Little Me invoked the Masculine One at Maw's, saving her many times, and that Sick and Tired emerged at Joanie's more than I knew before. Together, they tried to protect her as best they could, although I suppose that in hindsight, Little Me would not have created someone who thought that ending it all would protect her.

Dr. Townes decided not to put me into the Safe Room. It was just as well; I had enough to talk about on the outside and hoped I wouldn't have to traverse that Victorian house again so soon. He handed me the journal from the previous week, and I handed him the new one from The Chatterbox. I explained to him that no one else seemed interested in contributing to the journal, and he said that it was important that I try to include everybody, most especially Little Me. He said again that Little Me was the best part of me, she had been silenced for too long, and one of the journals was actually for her to express herself.

The Chatterbox became indignant. "I'm the one who speaks for the rest of us. I am the one who has honed the writing skill to express what needs to be said. Isn't that why I was created, after all?"

I had to interject. "That may be true, but you're not the only one with a voice around here."

Dr. Townes began to take notes, writing quickly as though he was my secretary taking dictation. He seemed fascinated by the discussion I was having with The Chatterbox. "I'm intrigued with how quickly you switch from one to another," he said.

The Perfectionist moved quickly to the front. "Haven't you ever talked to yourself before, Doctor?"

I blushed when I realized that it was the Perfectionist who had perfected the art of the facetious, cheekily admonishing him for his apparent ignorance in such matters. Townes found her delightful, nonetheless, as he smiled wryly and continued taking notes. He asked whether I experienced any pain other than the pain I described during my sessions.

"Except for Little Me, there isn't much pain, although I do feel pressure in my head when someone else is in front." I explained that the pain was greatest when Little Me was out in front, and that it seemed the others only pained me if they were forceful in their movements to the front, or whenever there were arguments and disagreements among them.

Apparently bored with my discussion with the therapist, The Chatterbox interrupted. "Joanie did some really nasty things. Did you read the part where she put a spoon down Baby Justin's diaper while he was trying to crawl up the stairs to the dining room? We saw that in the Safe Room."

While The Chatterbox rattled on, I remembered Sick and Tired and that I needed to air her issues or suffer the early morning wake up calls again. I moved back into position in front and interrupted The Chatterbox. Townes listened intently as I told him about Sick and Tired keeping me up at night. I was also concerned that my behavior with them in tow was becoming increasingly more erratic and difficult to explain away to friends and family.

"May I speak with Sick and Tired directly?" he asked. I searched but couldn't find her. I asked The Chatterbox if she was near her, because I couldn't feel her.

That's peculiar, I thought. She was always there, just below the surface, but today, I couldn't find Sick and Tired anywhere. It had to be the medication, I explained to Townes. Perhaps the increased dosage had pushed her even farther away from the surface.

"I'm so annoyed, and confused, too. The medicine is supposed to be helping me, but it is keeping me awake because Sick and Tired keeps me up much too much! I guarantee she will surface early in the damn morning tomorrow! I can't sleep!" Even as I griped, I was irritated because I realized Sick and Tired could get through only when the medication was at its weakest, which was early in the morning.

Townes remained silent for a moment, as though in thought, and then looked at me above his glasses, the way he looked at me when he wanted to be the most reassuring.

"Trust me, she won't be going away, not anytime soon. She is a part of the whole. Remember that. True, the medication is keeping her back, because she is that part of the whole who is depressed and the medication works best on that part. When we are in the Safe Room, she will be able to express herself to a much greater extent. She can hear me, so I will say to her, 'You are not going anywhere, there is too much work left to do for your healing.'" He got up from his chair and walked over to me. He placed his hand on my shoulder and patted it gently. "You'll be fine." I hoped to God that what he said to her was enough to get me a good night's sleep for a change.

The one-hour session was over according to the clock under the table near Dr. Townes' chair. He got up and walked to his desk to write down my next appointment in his book. "Next week, same time?"

"Yep," I said, and headed home. When I checked my phone, I discovered that my husband, my children, and my boss had called me. I wanted to ignore them all, so I deleted them—only allegorically, of course, and only from my missed calls.

On the drive home, scores of thoughts crowded my mind, moving around like musical chairs, stopping at a point, as though each thought required a specific place in my head and wouldn't allow others to rest in the same spot. Each thought wanted to get top attention, but many were too vague to understand. One thing was certain, though—there was so much more to talk about, so much more to write about. I was going to ask Little Me to journal this time. Even though I respected The Chatterbox for her ability to communicate for the group, Little Me knew firsthand about the events of her young life, and I knew I needed to get through that part before I could move on. I would go home, kiss the hubby, take about eight ibuprofen tablets, enjoy a good shower, eat, and then sit her down at my desk to write. That was the plan.

Chapter Fifteen

I was pleased that there was no objection from The Chatterbox when I asked Little Me to write in the journal. When I asked for Little Me, I felt painful sensations in my skull again, which felt like something hit it HARD. Little Me was in out in front and had taken full control of my body. As I observed how she wrote, I had to abruptly interrupt. As smart as she was, she was still too young to write legibly, at least for now.

"That's funny!" I chuckled. I certainly wasn't aware that allowing Little Me full control meant just that; even my handwriting. Although still in pain, we both decided that I should do the writing, and that she would dictate. That was most undoubtedly doable, we agreed, and I took two more ibuprofen tabs.

"I love Nana. Nana loved me," Little Me began, in earnest, as I picked up the pen to write. "My brother used to fight me. He used to make me cry all the time. He was so mean. He liked to punch me in my stomach, so I couldn't breathe!"

I interrupted her again. We needed some consistency. Perhaps if I asked questions, then she could respond instead of aimlessly speaking as thoughts occurred. I decided that the best course would be to interview her with direct questions. I thought that by starting with my mother, we could create a premise for the journal writing. "Little Me, how did you feel about Mommy?"

"I love my Mommy. She would leave me in the house by myself sometimes because she had to go to work. She hurt herself at work because she worked with big machines that cut her fingers."

To my surprise, I remembered that. *Oh my, no repression there*, I thought.

Little Me continued. "When she left me by myself, sometimes I would make tents and make camp fires." *That must have been blocked*, I thought. I didn't remember that.

"You made fires in the house?" I asked, confused by the notion. "Little Me, I don't recall those fires. You say you were making campfires?"

"Oh, yes," she said. I was writing feverishly, and trying to comprehend at the same time. I wondered if this line of questioning would be better served in the Safe Room. I wrote as Little Me recounted, "I was cooking sometimes. I like to cook. Spaghetti, mostly; because if you put it in water it gets all shriveled and thick and looks like Nanny's and Mommy's spaghetti."

I needed to get deeper into the fire starting. She didn't seem to understand where I was going with my questioning. "What made you start the first fire?" I inquired.

"I liked to look at the colors in the fire. I struck a match the first time and stared at the fire. It was pretty, but it didn't last long enough, so I struck another, then another, but none of them lasted long enough. When I put a little piece of toilet paper on the floor and struck a match on it, it floated up into the air on fire and then floated back down like a feather. That was fun to see. When it floated back down, it went out, and when I touched the tissue, it turned to black powder."

"You mean ashes," the Perfectionist corrected.

Little Me continued, "It just never lasted long enough, so I ran downstairs to get the whole roll of toilet tissue, or sometimes I would get magazines or newspapers and tear them into little pieces, light them and watch them float. One time, though, I got really scared, because I had a big fire that whooshed up to the top of the ceiling instead of floating. I had to run downstairs to the bathroom to get a bucket of water to put it out. When I did, it stunk up the house with smoke, and I had to cover the floor with a rug to hide the big burn that the fire put on the floor. When my Mommy got home, she said, 'I smell smoke.' I was so happy she didn't come upstairs to see what I did, because I would get a real good beating for that. I made a lot of fires in my room. I made so many fires that you could see all the burns in the floor where I made them, small black spots and big black spots. But Mommy never even noticed them. Mommy never caught me. Neither did Nanny. When my brother was home, he only let me make campfires sometimes. He didn't like fire the same way I did, so he would throw water on them too soon, before the paper even had a chance to float most of the time."

My fingers were cramping. I had to take a break, although I didn't want to, since Little Me was opening up, and I was getting some good stuff for the therapist to sort through. I was glad that I decided to take a long weekend, so I would have much more time to devote to writing in the journal. I thanked Little Me and asked her to remember some more things, and told her we would get back together to collaborate soon. I turned out the lights and kissed my husband, who was already asleep. It was midnight, and I was exhausted.

I woke up the next morning feeling refreshed. Just as the therapist assured me, I didn't hear from Sick and Tired all night, although she was back again, just below the surface and I could feel her. *I haven't taken the day's medication yet,* I thought. I acknowledged her as I walked past the desk where I left the journal. Looking at the journal and thinking about Little Me, I thought, *I am going to get right back to you.* I left my room, and then walked down to the kitchen to make some tea.

The wonderful aroma of freshly brewed herbal tea met me like an old, trusted friend not seen in years. I hastily poured a full mug and ran back upstairs, careful not to spill most of it. *I have all day today,* I thought. I thumbed through the journal to find a new page to start and was surprised to learn I had written twenty pages the night before.

My head started to pound again, and my skull began to feel raw and trounced upon, the cue that Little Me was moving up front. Once in front, she dived right back into her recollections, though not quite where she left off.

"My Mommy liked to drink whiskey; Dewar's White Label Scotch. Sometimes Nanny and Mommy would drink a whole lot of it in the kitchen with other people. She was so funny when she drank, and I liked her a whole lot better when she was drunk, because she laughed and played with us more." I wrote quickly as her thoughts merged into my own recollections.

"When Mommy drank, she would tickle us. She would sing 'I love you, pork chop— don't let me eat you—' and chase my brother and me all around the house. Then when she caught us, she would tickle us so hard that we laughed until we had to pee." I remembered fondly and smiled.

Little Me continued. "Sometimes when Mommy drank, she would fall and hurt herself. I would cry, because I hated when she hurt herself. She broke her ankle one time and needed a wheelchair. The only good part was if she was on the warpath, she couldn't come up the stairs fast enough to beat us if our room was dirty. We would have time to pick up our stuff off the floor and make our beds before she got upstairs. By then she couldn't beat us, only threaten us with future beatings if she caught the room dirty."

I took a short bathroom break and returned. I cracked the cramp out of my writing hand and thanked Little Me for her perseverance. She was still raring to continue.

"Mommy had a boyfriend named Mr. Robert. He was the one who lived in the house with us. He liked us and used to take us to Atlantic City to the beach to play in the water. Sometimes he would take us on the rides, too. I liked him. The only time I didn't like him was when he beat up Mommy and that would make me cry so hard. When they would fight it would always be late at night, and the sounds always scared me. Every time I heard thumping or heavy sounds like something hard falling, I thought they were fighting. I would cover my head in the covers so I couldn't hear the noise, but I could always hear it anyway. One time when I heard them fighting, I ran downstairs to save Mommy from him, and saw her bleeding from her nose. Her lip was bruised and swollen up. She had a black eye. One time she chased him out of the house with a gun and stood guard at the front door with it. And one time, I jumped on his back when he was on top of my Mommy, punching on her, and he threw me against the wall in the hallway."

"Men," I sighed. At once I began questioning my own choices in men. I felt like I was treading on some precarious ground and felt a bit uneasy. I never thought about any of it before, but perhaps there was some sort of resentment over my mother's choices that lurked somewhere inside not yet explored. I asked Little Me, hoping she could shed a little light on it, since she brought up my mother's live-in boyfriend.

"Little Me," I asked, "What did you think about Mommy's boyfriends?" Suddenly, my pencil began to scratch the surface of the paper, until it scraped a long, deep tear directly through the spot where I was writing. The Masculine One was controlling the pencil, obviously agitated by my question.

"I'm sorry. That must be a sore subject, I guess," I said. "Let's talk about something else." I tried to console the Masculine One.

Little Me did not respond. *What did I do*? I thought. My head became obscured by a cloud of ambiguity, in much the same way that it did whenever the Masculine One was near. My hands quaked, my headache subsided somewhat, and I began writing hastily, as my pencil moved rapidly, furiously across the paper. The Masculine One had moved her way to the front and was writing as she spoke.

"Let's see, there was Mr. Lynn, the fat drunk, who drove the red Cadillac. He always wore dark suits and ties, had red eyes and liked to drink corn liquor. Actually, any liquor would do for him. The smell of liquor oozed from his pores and mixed with that nasty cheap cologne he wore to try to mask it. On any given day, he either met her at a bar, picked her up to take her to a bar, or he came to the house and then they all got drunk together in the kitchen. I think that mom drank the most when he was around.

"There was the Crater Head," The Masculine One continued. "Little Me named him Crater Head because he was bald and had dents and dings in his head, much like a full moon on a clear night. He was another drunk with red eyes and stinky breath, except that his eyes were large and beady.

"Mr. Roland wore Russian hats; the black kind, boxy and made of Persian lamb. He was handsome. Little Me didn't know much about him, except that he used to come to Mom's job and that's where Little Me used to see him sometimes."

As the Masculine One wrote, I recalled Mr. Lynn, Crater, and Mr. Roland, having seen each on different occasions. I would simply speak politely and go about my way whenever I saw them. I never really gave them much thought otherwise.

I really didn't want the Masculine One to overpower the journal writing, because Little Me was supposed to be doing it. But when the Masculine One was in front and fully engaged, she was unyielding, so I knew there was no use resisting.

The Masculine One continued, "There was one other man that Little Me can remember, but not by name. Little Me didn't trust him. He left her in a car with her brother for a long time while he went to some bar under a railroad trellis. She didn't like him because she knew that he and Mom were having sex. Little Me walked in on them once. She hated him for that, and she hated Mom, too."

The Masculine One suddenly retreated from the front, causing me to drop the pencil to the floor. I rushed back to the front and quickly closed the journal. Hopefully, we were finished for a while.

When I got to work the next day, there was a memo in my in-box from my boss. He wanted to see me immediately, but that was all that I read. The rest was just a blur. I walked into his office, expecting the worse, inasmuch as my behavior over the last few months certainly warranted at least a scolding, and at most, a verbal warning. I got neither. A nice boss that I had, he was only concerned with my well being and sincerely wondered if I needed to take time off; that perhaps the stress of the job had finally gotten to me. I definitely thought better of telling him anything about my situation but thanked him, nonetheless, for his kindness. I wasn't interested in taking a leave of absence; the stress from the job was actually a welcome respite from the insanity I lived daily everywhere else.

"The hardest thing about facts is facing them ..."

Chapter Sixteen

Week Twenty-nine

I was extremely anxious about giving the journal to Dr. Townes. Rushing from the car, I scooped the journal from the seat, almost forgetting my purse. I ran to the door, and to my surprise, it was locked. I knocked, once, twice, harder, and more frantically with each knock, until he peeked his head from his office door. It was 4:15. I knew I was early, but I was willing to wait. Perhaps I would even brew some tea using his new water cooler. He shut the office door behind him and walked toward the locked entrance.

"We have had some not so savory people entering the building," he whispered as he let me in. "Our security system is not working properly, so we're locking the door until it's repaired. I hope you weren't concerned."

Of course I was, but I felt better knowing I would have my session. I had a great deal to discuss with him.

"I have a lot in the journal for you to read, but I don't even know if I want you to read it. I'll just give them to you," I said, and tried to shove them into his hands.

He placed his forefinger in front of his mouth and silently shushed me; there was still a patient in his office. Slightly embarrassed, I walked over to my favorite seat near the old sports and travel magazines, politely waiting for my turn. As usual, another patient's time spilled into mine, but I didn't complain as she left, and I walked in. I kept the Perfectionist from blurting; she wanted to utter something curt to both the woman and Dr. Townes for their tardiness, something I was sure I would have to apologize for later. I handed over the journals and flopped onto the couch. Then I took off my shoes and made myself comfortable. "You're going to have some really interesting reading today, Doc," I said.

He placed the books on the end table near his chair, took his glasses out of his pocket, and slowly placed them on his face. "How did it feel allowing Little Me to speak?"

I shrugged and told him I didn't know, except that it felt very strange, with painful sensations that were difficult to describe. I said that my skull felt like someone bashed me in the head with a mallet when I knew she was in front, and that it was confusing because it was me, but wasn't. "You know?" I asked.

He smiled and said, "She's wonderful. I love her. She is the best, simply the best." His comment was not what I expected, and I hated those comments about Little Me, so I shrugged them off as best as I could.

Dr. Townes requested that only Sick and Tired accompany us upstairs in the Victorian house since it was more difficult for Sick and Tired to resist participating when she was in the Safe Room. I was pleased she didn't struggle and seemed content to go along with the day's expedition. Townes asked the three of us to walk down the hallway and tell him how many doors there were. I could see one slightly cracked door straight ahead, revealing a small amount of light from the other side. He instructed us to walk toward the door and open it. Suddenly I was at the door to Nanny's bedroom, at Nanny's house as it was for most of my childhood and adolescence. I was beside the hallway closet where Nanny had placed a pair of curtains for doors to hide old clothes and anything else she needed to keep away from view. There I was, alone with Sick and Tired because Little Me had disappeared once again. I looked around the hallway. A foreboding coursed through me; I was nervous at the prospect that yet another predicament would threaten Little Me, and that I still had more repressed memories waiting to be untapped. I was afraid to open the door.

"Where are you?" Townes asked. I didn't want to answer. "Have you gone through the hallway?"

"Yes," announced Sick and Tired. I tried to silence her, to no avail. So many times, Little Me would disappear, and then I would get slammed with some repressed memory. I had no reason to believe anything would be different this time. I also knew it was pointless attempting to hush any of the others, each having learned early how to speak through my mouth with or without my consent, in or out of the Safe Room. It was all very bizarre, given that they were all identified by now. At any given moment, they were working my lips, my hands, and my entire body. They were deciding what I should wear, and were saying things or behaving in ways that, before therapy, used to make me wonder, *why the hell did I do that?* Or, *what the heck did I just say that for?*

Sick and Tired answered, "We are in Nana's hallway upstairs, at her bedroom door." I suppose Dr. Townes sensed that I was nervous, especially since Sick and Tired answered him instead of me.

Once again, he tried to console me, but his consolation and reassurances were worthless by now. Still, in his most fatherly voice, he said, "Little Me is not really experiencing anything now, and you will be all the better for the experience. Don't be afraid to open the door."

I slowly but cautiously opened the door to Nanny's bedroom, just a crack.

Through the small crack, I caught a quick glimpse of Nanny's bed and observed large legs, small legs, a couple of shoes, and tiny little feet thrashing about. I heard laughing, as well as muffled screams. There were also stifled cries, as though someone were gagged. I suddenly became short of breath. I couldn't breathe. I gasped for air, but none would come. I slammed the door and ran down the hallway in the opposite direction. I was sweating profusely. There was no door back to the Safe Room, and I felt faint.

"Help, I can't breathe!" I pleaded with Dr. Townes. "I don't want to go in there! I don't want to go in there!" I felt a sharp pain deep inside my body, like a knife slicing through my heart as though it was a slab of bacon at a butcher shop. I fell to my knees on the floor, clutching my chest. Then I felt someone close to me. "Will someone please get me out of here?" I cried. It was Sick and Tired trying to calm me, which was certainly peculiar for her. "I need to leave. Please ask Dr. Townes to bring us out." I pleaded with Sick and Tired to help me get out of there and back into the Safe Room with the angels. It was too much for me to take in. Something was happening in there that I preferred not to know.

Seeing how distraught I looked, Sick and Tired asked Townes if we could return to the Safe Room, but he didn't respond. She turned to me and said that I would have to face what was happening. Once faced, she said I could throw it away, or just leave it to her to deal with. I wasn't buying that argument. We were in a place where I had to deal with these revelations on my own, in my own way. I knew the only reason Sick and Tired was with me was because she was in that room with Little Me when whatever happened, happened. She knew what I was in for.

I picked myself up off the floor, holding onto the rickety wooden railing for support. I caught my breath and turned to face Nanny's bedroom. Then I walked slowly to the door, like a good soldier knowing she was about to die but going into battle anyway. I closed my eyes, not at all ready to look inside, but swung the door wide open nonetheless.

I heard the sounds of laughter, whispering, and then I heard the muffled sounds of screaming and crying. I opened my eyes and looked on Nanny's bed. Her old fashioned, chenille bedspread with the fringe all around was on the floor. The sheets and pillows were strewn around the perimeter of the bed from the rustling and thrashing of arms, feet, torsos, and legs. My brother was there, looking strangely at Little Me, holding down her legs as she struggled, squirming to be let go. She looked about eight or nine years old. There were my cousins, the fat one and the skinny one from Nanny's side of the family, the children of the uncle that my mom went to live with when she ran away to New York. There they were, one holding Little Me's mouth and one on top of her, naked and grinding on her tiny body. They were laughing, making sport of Little Me as she lay there crying. The Fat One, who'd been on top, finished and lifted himself off Little Me, leaving a trail of semen on her legs and vaginal area. Little Me screamed in horror when she saw the disgusting trail.

"Aw that's nothin' but dog water!" said the cousin who was holding Little Me's mouth. "That won't get you pregnant." Little Me's gasps and frantic screams that she was going to get pregnant filled the air. There really wasn't any way Little Me could get pregnant, since at eight years old she had not yet had her period. Both cousins agreed with each other, with Edward looking on intently, as if he was learning a valuable lesson.

"Dog water is what we get first," said the Fat One. "Then we get the other stuff that can make you pregnant. Dog water can't get you pregnant."

Self-righteous and secure in their ignorance of their bodily fluids, they nodded in agreement. Little Me wiped herself off with part of the sheet that was left on the bed and dropped the sticky, smelly sheet on the floor. She put her head down and left the room. Sick and Tired and I followed her out and shut Nanny's bedroom door behind us. Then the door to the entrance of the Safe Room appeared, and we entered. Little Me looked up at me, but I couldn't speak. I was too filled with anger at the latest epiphany that invaded my consciousness. I realized that Little Me was the one, not the others, who had been concealing things from me. She had collected all my hurt and hoarded all my pain, only sharing parts of it with others. I just couldn't understand why she kept it all from me. I was more confused than ever.

When we entered the Safe Room, I was never so happy to see Jesus waiting there. I welcomed Him into me with open arms after Little Me and Sick and Tired disappeared into Him.

When I returned to his office, Townes was seated in his chair, writing zealously, trying to get it all down on paper. I was sure he was going to have a busy night, what with reading the journals and with all he had to go over from today's session. I was exhausted, and thankful when the Masculine One offered to drive, explaining that there were too many crazy drivers on the long ride, and that she was the best one to handle them. I suspected she was actually showing uncharacteristically genuine compassion when she offered. When I got home, I was too tired to cook and suggested my husband eat takeout. Then I dragged myself upstairs and fell into bed.

"There were other things, you know." A low whisper from deep within beckoned me to inquire as I rested in bed, awake, but with my eyes closed. I didn't want to hear it and knew that if I entertained the whisper, I would get more flashbacks.

"I'm in the body; you can't ignore that." The whisper grew louder. I turned in the bed, on my right side, and fluffed my pillow under my head, still trying desperately to ignore the voice. It sounded like The Chatterbox, but I wasn't certain. Surely there couldn't be someone I still hadn't met.

"Hey! Why are you trying to ignore the obvious? I said there were other things. Do you want to wait an entire week or do you want something to put into the journal now?" I recognized the voice. I glanced up at the clock on the wall and noticed it was not yet midnight. Although I wasn't in any mood to write in the journal and was still angry with Little Me for repressing important memories, I got up halfheartedly, retrieved other the journal from my pocketbook on the night table, and sat at the desk. I opened the book to a fresh page, one of very few left, and then paused, pencil in hand.

"Okay, so what else happened to me that I should write into this journal?" I quipped. "Should I prepare for another massive skull ache and wait for Little Me to come out front to tell me another crazy story, or are you going to grace me tonight?" There was no response. I asked smugly, "Was that inappropriate?" No one responded. *Hmmm*, I thought, *she seems so eager to chatter up a storm. Perhaps I angered her when I mentioned Little Me, but after all, Townes did say Little Me should be the one using the journal.*

I waited patiently at first and then grew more impatient. There I sat, my left hand holding up my head, my right hand holding the pencil. I stared at the open journal, at the blank page, waiting for the words to come. There were no words. It was as though someone plugged a huge hole in the dam to keep the water inside from pouring out.

Who's in control here? I thought, feeling irritated and helplessly frustrated. Then suddenly, a wave of extreme vulnerability swept me, leaving me more perplexed about myself than ever, if such a thing were even possible. I wanted to be angry, but with whom? And for what purpose would it serve to be angry with one's selves? How ridiculous a prospect and how utterly crazy had I become, even entertaining the thought of really having the condition my therapist told me I had. Were there actually other personas inextricably tied together in my head, separate but not, together but not? I was out of control of my own mind, and I had to get it back somehow.

I got up from the chair, walked over to the bed and stood there, staring blankly. I was determined to go to bed, and I was going to be the one to decide if I would go to sleep. I was determined to control something for myself about myself. I stood there, staring at the bed, wondering if I would really get any sleep. I got in and slid the covers over my head, adamant about getting some sleep and listening to no one. I closed my eyes, expecting the worst but hoping for the best.

Morning brought me no closer to a sense of assurance about my place inside my head, although it seemed I managed to sleep the entire night. I had fewer answers and more questions for the therapist, more issues that had to be resolved, or I was going to stop therapy altogether.

When I arrived at work, Marissa was hungry for more information about my sessions, but I found my mental situation becoming progressively thornier, details of which were definitely not the sort of stuff to feed her so early in the morning. Instead, we sat in her office over the coffee and bagels she brought in for us, while I made small talk, thankful that The Chatterbox was in retreat.

I wrestled inside while the Masculine One and Sick and Tired argued over whether I should let my friend in on their existence. "I do not care how fucking close you are, she will back off when she finds out about us," the Masculine One said. Her argument was plausible. Frankly, the thought of telling my family was frightful enough, what with the revelations of late. How could I think Marissa would understand, or for that matter, accept, if I was afraid my family wouldn't? I decided not to tell her any more than what I thought she could take, without giving her rise to dig deeper, and then I decided to take a few days off.

Chapter Seventeen

Over the next few days at home, their collective silence was more conspicuous than the chatter was before. It seemed I got angry when any of them emerged and then just as angry when they were all quiet. There was no consensus to be reached among us, and the level of torment was overwhelming for me. I began to suspect that someone was muffling Little Me but couldn't figure out who it might be. The Chatterbox apparently was stifled somehow as well. I decided to write in the journal myself. I had memories. Not everything was blocked.

"To hell with them," I thought aloud, just in case they cared to know that I was thoroughly annoyed. I walked into the bathroom to throw some water on my face and to brush my teeth and noticed a small amount of blood when I brushed. *Gingivitis*, I thought.

"Shhhhh," a voice began, "Don't think about anything right now, not even your gums," The voice whispered. It was The Chatterbox. I listened, trying to oblige her by not thinking of anything but understanding how difficult that was, having tried many times in vain to do it before.

"This is absurd. I have to think in order to listen," I said.

She whispered again, "No. You do not. Just keep your mind on me right now so I can take over. I have a great deal to write in the journal, things that Little Me blocked." She continued, "She is having second thoughts about letting you in on any more life experiences. But my job is to keep us informed no matter what, since you brought us out."

I quickly wiped my mouth and ran back to the desk where my pencil and the journal were, undisturbed from before. Acquiescence was my only alternative, knowing how unrelenting The Chatterbox could be; therefore, I allowed The Chatterbox to write through my hands once again.

"I never thought of myself as having been molested, not until now," she began to write while I read. "My brother and I used to do it all the time. You know, sex. I don't even know when it started; so don't stop me to ask. We also used to spit on the walls and race the spit as it traveled down. I'm saying that because we did a lot of really stupid things together. Most of the time, I would call him upstairs to our room because I *wanted* to do it. I was probably the instigator most of the time."

The words sounded like they were coming from Little Me, but I didn't have a skull ache, as I did whenever she was in front. I needed to stop The Chatterbox for a moment to take in what I was reading, if only I could stop her. "For the love of God, I need to ask just one question," I pleaded. The Chatterbox continued writing while I watched and read, helpless to control my own fingers and sorry that I allowed her to take control in the first place.

Having sex with my brother sounded reprehensible to me. There was simply no way I could have wanted to have sex with my own brother. That notion was patently absurd. Besides, I never liked sex. Sex was the Trollop's department, and she didn't even like it, either. She'd said that herself when I met her in the Safe Room for the first time.

"I did it with my skinny cousin, too," The Chatterbox continued. "He was my favorite cousin, and I wanted to marry him when I grew up. He was always so gentle and kind to me, and he didn't hurt me. It was okay to have sex with him."

This was impossible to believe. After that episode in the Safe Room when I watched the two of them raping Little Me, how could she feel that way about either of them? That thinking was perverted; just nasty. I was definitely going to have to discuss this with Dr. Townes, and I wasn't going to wait until he had a chance to read these journal entries. I pleaded with The Chatterbox to allow me to control my thoughts, if only for a moment. My hand was cramping from writing without rest for hours.

Suddenly, my hand stopped and fell limply on the journal. The pencil dropped from my fingers and rolled onto the floor. The Chatterbox admonished, “You have to stop thinking. You are distracting me from journaling. There is much to write down, and it needs to flow properly. You are always blocking me! Stop blocking me!”

Of course, it was undoubtedly my intention to block The Chatterbox. I wanted her to stop. I was shocked by what I was reading. Little Me was a cute little thing with her ponytails and fish mouth smile. The girl The Chatterbox was talking about was disgusting. She was nasty and wretched. I didn’t like the person The Chatterbox was talking about; I hated her, and so it couldn’t be Little Me. The Chatterbox was fabricating the whole thing. It was as simple as that.

I picked up the pencil from the floor, thankful for the brief respite from writing, and snatched the opportunity to speak. “Why are you telling me these lies?” I asked, half hoping The Chatterbox would laugh it off as some ridiculous prank. “I told you, Little Me is having second thoughts about you. She doesn’t think you are strong enough to survive it all.” The Chatterbox went on to explain that Little Me didn’t want any of it to come out in the Safe Room because she was too ashamed.

“I’ve gone insane for real,” I cried. I stared at myself through the mirror on my vanity table and sobbed. “I’ve lost my mind, in real life! Certifiably crazy! There are voices talking in my head! I have voices talking to me in my head! I’m a schizophrenic!”

“Mom picked Little Me’s friends.” The Chatterbox took the pencil and started to write again. I didn’t want to read anymore and closed my eyes while she wrote. Undaunted by any attempts to ignore her, The Chatterbox wrote and droned on. “Mommy was strict like that. She picked Barbara Jean, who lived in an apartment next door. Barbara Jean’s bedroom wall was on the other side of Little Me’s bedroom wall. Barbara Jean was a lot older than her and could fight. Sometimes when they were each home alone, they talked through the wall. One day, Mommy allowed Barbara Jean to baby-sit for Little Me. They were playing in her room. It was dark outside and she turned off the light. Barbara Jean pulled down her panties and lay on the edge of the bed, with her legs spread wide open at the bottom. Barbara Jean told Little Me to put her head down into her private parts. Little Me told her that she didn't want to, and told her no, so she grabbed Little Me's head and pushed it into her crotch and started gyrating. She got so angry when Little Me refused to cooperate with her, and smacked her in her face and punched her in the stomach. She beat her up, even though the Masculine One fought her hard. Barbara Jean was just too strong. Little Me never told Mommy though. She never told anybody until now. Mommy thought that Barbara Jean was a nice young lady and made her one of Little Me's friends. Just goes to show you, moms aren't always the best judges of character.

"By the time Little Me was in Junior high school, she decided to be a virgin, just took it upon herself. Virginity was the talk in school among the girls: who was a virgin, who wasn't, who got their cherry busted, and who didn't. It was important for Little Me to be a virgin. Little Me was ashamed to admit that she was not, because the girls who weren't virgins had bad reputations from the boys in school. So, she became a virgin again, and while her girlfriends were having sex with their boyfriends, she wouldn't, and when they got pregnant, she didn't."

I was numb from what I heard. I could have jabbed myself between the ears with my pencil and not have felt the impact or the blood. Why would The Chatterbox make up such horrible stories and hoist them all onto Little Me like that? The Little Me that I met months ago was a tiny, wide-eyed, wonderful little girl. She was pure, sweet, and untarnished. She could not possibly have been involved in such disgusting affairs. The child I was reading about was damaged goods, a wretch, and an anti-societal pariah. What I had just read was The Chatterbox's ravings. It was Little Me's fiasco, not mine.

None of this nonsense can be true, I thought as I shook my head in disbelief. In unison, the Perfectionist, Sick and Tired, the Trollop, and the Masculine One all said that everything was true, then said no more on the subject for the night.

Week Thirty-one

The days at work were melting into each other, and I was finding my ability to concentrate on the demands each day increasingly untenable. I was tempted to take my boss' advice and take a leave of absence. At every turn, it seemed there was some measure of crud and filth oozing out of the cracks and crevices in that so-called Safe Room, and the ooze was threatening to fill my home as well. I understood Sick and Tired's assessment of life as she saw it. The muck was so thick that I was suffocating, and that same muck was threatening to destroy my home and my family. I was going to ask Townes if he could give me a note for work, so I could get some time off and wouldn't lose my job.

I was relieved when the Perfectionist offered to dress me. I was an emotional wreck and couldn't think past the last moment when I had a thought, let alone choose anything to wear on my own. When I arrived at Townes' office, he was preoccupied with something for my entire session, which was a blessing in disguise. He said that an unusual session earlier in the day had extinguished his energy and apologized for appearing somewhat distant. I tried to put on a pleasant face but found it very difficult to hide my feelings.

He asked me about my day, and we engaged in our usual banter before the session began in earnest. I asked if I could stay out of the Safe Room, fearing that what was written in the journal would become painfully visible. He was completely lost in his own thoughts, and it was apparent that I would not have to go into the Safe Room after all. I handed him the journal on my way out of the door and was relieved that the visit ended as uneventfully as it began.

Good, I thought. *Another blessing in disguise*. I got into the car and the Masculine One drove us home. On my way to bed, I remembered that I forgot to get the note for work.

Chapter Eighteen

Week Thirty-two

I was embarrassed before I even walked into Townes' office. I knew by now he'd read the journal's latest sordid entries.

Before I could get into the waiting room, he motioned for me to come into his office, and he immediately began to discuss the journal.

"You had such a really, really rough time of it." He tried to both sympathize and comfort. "Do you have any idea of the severity of trauma you experienced? On a scale of one to ten, where ten is the worst, I would have to put you at a nine. In my view, the only other patient of mine whose trauma was worse than yours was a woman whose father tied her up in the bathroom because it aroused him sexually. Frankly, and I don't say this to many patients, you made me cry."

I was mortified but could only hold my head down and shrug. I decided that he definitely wasn't talking about me. He was talking about Little Me. Why was he telling me he cried? Embarrassment swept over my entire body and engulfed me like the flames of the Masculine One's fiery presence in the Safe Room.

"That wasn't very professional!" whispered the Perfectionist to me. "Perhaps he thought he was talking to Little Me."

"That's it," I said. "You're talking to me, Doctor, not Little Me." Then I backed off to allow the Perfectionist to handle Townes. She would be better prepared for his comments and could step toe to toe with him.

The Perfectionist shrugged and sighed, then responded to him, "I was no worse off than some who were worse off than me. How can you sit there as a professional and compare me to another patient to my face, no less?"

The Masculine One rose to the surface and chimed in, "What do you mean severity? There are people a whole lot worse off. My life was no less normal than anybody else's. You always want me to think my life was so bad. You have some goddamn nerve! I hate you!"

Ordinarily, Townes would look at me through the top of his glasses, and using his most reassuring voice, he would talk me down. Today, he was stern, like a father scolding a child for being obstinate. He said he thought he was speaking to Little Me and realized he wasn't. He apologized for the comparison, but we all felt his comments weren't appropriate under any circumstances, whether he thought he was talking to Little Me or not.

"I thought I was speaking to Little Me, and I'm not. I want to speak to her," he said. His tone was short, as though irritated with me.

I didn't want Little Me in front today. I wasn't prepared for the embarrassment that she caused me, or the massive aching in my skull. If the things that The Chatterbox wrote were true, and if the others were in agreement with me, then I didn't want Little Me around anymore. Perhaps we could just push her back deep inside as she was before I started the therapy. Perhaps I would just stop going to therapy altogether, a view I was certain would set well with the others.

He stared oddly at me, observed me more closely, and appeared concerned. He told me that my eyes had grown wide, and that I was sweating. I knew I was sweating but had hoped he wouldn't notice. He said that I looked like I was in some kind of distress, but I didn't feel distressed, only extremely confused. He left the office, came back with water from the water cooler in the waiting room, and handed it to me. He handed me a tissue from the table and then began to explain that he needed to speak with Little Me because she was the one who needed the therapy. "Little Me normalized life in order to cope," he said.

"That's absurd!" screamed the Perfectionist. Surprised by her sudden outburst, I held my mouth closed with my hand. Evidently, the Perfectionist was equally irritated with Townes and didn't want Little Me to come out front either.

"That's fucking crazy! You know what? I'm getting the hell of here. I told everybody that this stuff wasn't what it was cracked up to be," yelled the Masculine One.

I got up to walk out of the office but stopped just short of the door, as both the Perfectionist and the Masculine One argued with the therapist inside my head and outwardly through my mouth. There I stood, as reluctant a participant as I could possibly be, watching and listening as they argued with Dr. Townes, obviously stalling to keep Little Me from coming to the surface. I covered my ears and shook my head from side to side until I got dizzy.

Dr. Townes helped me back to my seat. The Masculine One suddenly eased into the background just below me, and the Perfectionist remained in front just above me.

I was in complete awe of the level of lunacy I had achieved at this point. I heard what Townes was telling me, but his statements begged a much bigger question. Certainly none of this was normal, and if I could understand anything, I could understand *that* unmistakably. As far as I was concerned, Little Me was *not* the *real me*. I couldn't stand the facts of her reality and wanted no part of them.

"Do you even know what normal is?" the Perfectionist asked Dr. Townes. "Futile attempts by doctors like you to answer that question are probably the basis for some of the most dreadful behavior perpetrated in the name of normal." She continued. "Someone else's hell might be my normal, or vice versa. Wouldn't you have to submit to that, Doctor?"

"What was written in that journal, that's her reality!" I screamed at him. "That is not my reality! I am nothing like Little Me, and no amount of normalization is going to convince me otherwise." I buried my head in my hands and sobbed.

Dr. Townes took off his glasses with a swipe. "Listen to me," he began, "let me explain something to you. You are as much her as you are you, the way you are today and the way you are dressed today. Little Me created you."

Little Me, WHAT? I asked myself, absolutely staggered by what I thought I had just heard. What was he saying? What nonsense was this? I glared at Townes, long and purposefully. I wanted him to know I was not buying what he was trying to sell.

I asked, "Dr. Townes, what did you just say?"

He looked at me directly in the eyes and repeated that Little Me created me, that I was one of *her* fragments, and that I was the reason why she had been repressing the memories.

"She repressed the memories from you, in order to live, and that is how *you* protected *her,*" he said.

Aghast, I sobbed uncontrollably into the tissues he handed me. The therapist continued to explain. "Each of you was created by Little Me to cope and to protect her in whatever way you could. You are all parts of her, and she is all of you, just spread apart for now. Our hope is to integrate all of Little Me's parts into one whole, and that includes you."

I was suddenly hurled back into the full front and unable to comprehend. "Wait a minute. I'm not real?" I sobbed. Was he telling me I wasn't real? Was this quack telling me that I was one of Little Me's insane creations? As I understood this experience, I had initiated it. I had embarked on this journey myself. When the therapist diagnosed me, he'd said I was fragmented. That meant Little Me was a fragment. I was fragmented, I thought, not a fragment myself. Wasn't I was the one who needed therapy because I was fragmented?

Little Me wasn't the one who solicited the therapist's name from my friend at work. I was the one who made the appointment, and I was the one who had to be healed and made whole. That was what this therapy was supposed to correct.

"Are you telling me that I am one of these fucking fragments created by Little Me; one of the figments of her warped imagination? One of her *coping* mechanisms? How can that be? Surely I'm not a fragment. Please tell me I'm real!" I sobbed. I was beside myself at the prospect that I was one of her figments, like the other figments in my head, and that this body wasn't even my own but hers, and that my mind wasn't my mind but hers. I didn't quite know how I was expected to fit in anymore, and I resented that Townes always called Little Me the best part of us. If any of this mess of my life was true, then she wasn't a damn part; she was actually the only legitimate one of us. *We were the illegitimates.* "I am not illegitimate! I couldn't have been created, not by some sniveling little snippet of a child with sanity issues."

I searched Dr. Townes' face for some reassurance but couldn't find any. Besides, it seemed clear he was only interested in Little Me and her well-being, not mine. "Doctor, how is she a part at all if she created me and the others as parts?" Tears streamed down my face.

As I gradually began to believe that what he was saying might indeed be true, Little Me started pressing on my skull. She was coming to the surface quickly, and I could tell she wanted to speak. *Humph*, I thought. *If she created me, then why am I able to control her comings and goings most times? And if I was created, then why didn't I get a name like the others when we all met in the Safe Room? What, then, is my cute little name? If she created me the way she created the others, then why do I hate her, if I was created by her to protect her? And why the fuck did she keep this insanity from me? From me! If I was created like the others, why was I kept in the dark, and the others knew me, but I didn't know them?*

The therapist got up from his chair and walked over to me, looking at me through the top of his glasses, which he had put back on, as he sat down next to me on the couch. I was trembling.

He put his hand on my shoulder. "Listen to me. You're as real as I am. Let me speak to Little Me now. I know she's waiting. Why don't we just let her come up front?" He patted my shoulder in his usual comforting way. Then suddenly, as though a dead weight had been placed on the top of my head, my head fell into my cleavage, with only the connection of the skin and bones from my neck holding it from rolling to the floor. The others had stopped ranting, and I felt exceptionally drained. I tried slowly to raise my head but couldn't lift my chin. Little Me was in front and in full control.

"You are the Gatekeeper," Little Me began. I struggled to maintain some semblance of composure as she continued. "You are my normal for the world to see."

The Gatekeeper? I thought. Little Me's explanation of my existence was no consolation and didn't erase the fact that I had my own feelings, with many of them hatred for her. I found it difficult to entertain the thought of being anything to Little Me anymore, let alone the Gatekeeper, for God's sake. My thoughts then drifted back to when I met the Masculine One for the first time, in the Safe Room, and she referred to meeting the *Gatekeeper* during therapy. "That was me, and I didn't even know it!" I screamed. I thought that the Masculine One was referring to someone I had yet to meet. Confusion hung onto me like a worn, weather-beaten shroud on an old, eccentric woman. Perhaps it was because my strength was so drained by Little Me in front; perhaps it was because I was finally finding out who I was and my position in her reality.

"Since I was the one in the dark all or most of the time, perhaps she should have named me 'Blissfully Ignorant.' I hate her," I retorted. My head felt so heavy, I had to lay my head against the arm of the couch for fear that it would really snap completely off my neck and roll onto the floor. Little Me looked at the therapist, as I listened and watched from inside.

"Everybody has a purpose. The Gatekeeper is my shield," said Little Me.

Dr. Townes nodded assuredly. "Yes. You created the Gatekeeper in order to shield yourself from feelings of shame. That shame was only exacerbated by your compounding guilt later. You were ashamed of yourself when Mr. Peace hurt you. You were ashamed of yourself when you were beaten and molested by Barbara Jean. You were ashamed when Bobby and your brother hurt you. The list just goes on. Creating the Gatekeeper afforded you another normal, one with which you didn't have to be ashamed. She didn't have to know any of the things you went through. The Gatekeeper could remain out of your reality, walking through your life with you, within the normal that she provided for you, the normal that helped you cope."

Dr. Townes took off his glasses and placed them on the end table. "The Gatekeeper is the face everyone sees, the one who coordinates the activities of the others. The beauty lies in the brilliance of her creation. Until therapy unlocked the doors in the Safe Room, your activities remained invisible. Your exquisite design was masterful. Little Me, you know it's completely plausible that the Gatekeeper hates what she knows about you now. Do you understand that, in essence, it's like hating yourself for being victimized? You don't have to hate yourself. You are a true survivor, not a victim anymore."

I listened, since that was the only thing I could do, and was having great difficulty digesting it all. It was an enormous amount of psychobabble to take in at one time, and I was surprised that Little Me seemed to understand much of what he meant. How could she allow me to think I was myself? How did she do it? Had I not begun this therapy, I quite possibly would never have discovered myself. It all seemed extremely unfair of her to keep me in the dark all these years. The therapist said that Little Me made much progress, although, at this point, I could only take his word for it.

Why don't I just defer everything to Little Me right now, and step back for good? I thought. For sure, Little Me was the loon, albeit brilliant, according to Townes. After all, I was only a figment of her masterful imagination. With all of the new information I was taking in, I had forgotten the original reason why I had begun therapy in the first place. Perhaps it really hadn't been my idea at all. Perhaps it had been Little Me whispering in my head. I looked over at the clock, which was placed strategically in front of the couch directly at eye view. The time was 5:35, and clear that my appointment was over.

I struggled to lift my head from the arm of the couch. It was easier now, but my skull still pained when I moved it. I was back out in front because Little Me stepped back, just right of the surface, still present but not interfering. I summoned the Masculine One to drive and started on the long trip home.

When I walked into the house, I threw my coat on the couch and ran upstairs. I sat at my vanity and stared at myself in the mirror, and then the shroud of confusion covered me once again. I was extremely ambivalent about my position in the grand persona that Little Me created. *If we were all together apart, then why did I feel so separated and whole by myself?* I thought. I stood still in the bedroom, which no longer even felt like my own. I looked over at the bed I slept in, and it no longer felt like mine. I thought about my husband, Victor. The man I lived with for so many years didn't even feel like my husband anymore.

Have these revelations caused me to split completely? I thought. I could feel Sick and Tired attempting to rise to the surface and struggled to keep her below me.

"Nonsense!" yelled the Masculine One. "Still, things would have been better if you hadn't gone into therapy to sort us out in the first place."

What in Heaven's name was I going to do? Therapy was supposed to help, but had apparently caused me to lose my mind. My friend went to the same doctor. She wasn't nuts. I was hearing voices I'd never heard before and discovered that some little person inside me was the mastermind behind my own existence, the mastermind behind my insanity and her own. If I was to believe that we were the same, then how could I reconcile my own independent thought?

"We need a meeting of the minds, so to speak," suggested The Chatterbox, apparently trying to lighten the air in the room. "Since we are all aspects of Little Me, let's call ourselves 'the Aspects,'" she said.

As ludicrous as an idea could be to design a club around the voices in one's head, I entertained the notion for a short while. *Why not*? I thought. The Aspects seemed as good a name as any. Besides, I was a bona fide lunatic.

"May the first meeting of the Aspects come to order?" I shouted facetiously into the air, as though in a huge chamber calling a boisterous crowd to attention. Victor, who had been downstairs watching television, ran upstairs. "What is going on? Are you okay? You have been acting crazy for a while now, and I am at my wit's end trying to figure you out!" he said, concerned by my progressively erratic behavior. I got up from the chair and threw myself onto the bed, sobbing uncontrollably.

Through all of the madness, it seemed my husband always appeared to take it in stride and was generally understanding, but I could tell he was having a hard time coping with my erratic behavior. Victor was often confused, but had concluded that his perceptions of me were of nothing more than menopausal mood swings. Not for one moment did he even entertain the thought that there were others to deal with as well, especially when one or more of them alternated. Their individual moods were like the difference between day and night, sunny and cloudy, dry and rainy. He lived through it all, and for so long. Apparently, Sick and Tired would take advantage of any sadness, misgivings, pain, or anguish, anything that she could detect from any one of us, and then behave miserably around him. Whenever he went out at night, Sick and Tired would move to the front to worry whether he was cheating. Then the Masculine One would leave him voicemail messages accusing him. The Perfectionist was always so picky and nagged him often about little things. The Masculine One always leapt out in front whenever any one of us got angry with him, or if he got angry with any one or all of us. Of course, there was always Big Fat, who loved how he ate and Victor raved about her cooking. One thing was absolutely certain. I knew that I loved him at least as much as Little Me or Mushy, maybe even more.

Victor never asked questions about therapy. He didn't even ask when it appeared I wasn't going anymore. He deserved to know the reasons why I'd started in the first place, but knowing what I knew about myself, Little Me, and the others, I was terrified he would find out just how crazy I was and leave me.

Nevertheless, I owed it to him to tell him everything, because he needed an explanation about what he had been dealing with since we got together sixteen years ago. I had to tell him how much I hated sex, but that it wasn't because of him. I had to tell him all about Mr. Peace, and the other things that Little Me kept hidden away. How in the absolute hell would one approach a discussion with one's spouse that he lived with about seven other women and one little girl, all wrapped together in one body? I was desperate to figure out the best way to tell him.

I ran into his arms, knocking him back against the dresser. "I'm sick, honey, really sick!" I sobbed. "I have other people inside my head talking to me and making decisions. I'm not even who I thought I was all these years!" I cried into his undershirt. "I'm the Gatekeeper for a little person inside me who created about seven others and me to cope with some trauma that she repressed. Evidently, I'm supposed to be that little girl; a part of her. She just decided that my job was to know absolutely nothing about anything except what I thought I knew, but everything I thought I knew were all lies! I'm not even myself! I don't have my own identity! I'm just part of hers!" I told him everything, expecting the worse but hoping for the best. His eyes grew wide and his mouth flung open and stayed there most of the time. I even explained that the night that he and I met, he'd actually met the Trollop, fresh out of a two and a half year ridiculous relationship with John the Baptist, a real schizophrenic. Surprisingly, the news of meeting the Trollop came as no surprise to him.

"I knew something was different back then," he said. He chuckled a little, while I searched his eyes for a glimpse of acceptance. I pulled him to me tightly, as closely as I could without suffocating him. Then he whispered, "I love you." He said he wasn't going to let himself be pushed away by Sick and Tired or the Masculine One, or any others who might be lurking inside, as yet unknown. He said that he would be with me through the rest of the work that had to be done, and that he would be with me long after the Little Me inside was fully healed.

"I told you, babe, I saw only black and white, and you made me see color. I'm with you forever." With that, he placed a tender peck on my lips with his and went back downstairs, as though we had just discussed the weather. The realization that my husband's genuine understanding and love apparently knew no bounds allowed me to relax slightly. I rested in my vanity chair to grab a morsel of quiet time, which was short lived.

"You started this shit!" shouted the Masculine One. "You just had to open up the can! Didn't think you'd find garbage in it, did you?" I closed my ears with my index fingers, sticking them inside as far as they could safely fit.

"Never should have gone in the first place!" said Sick and Tired. "Little Me should bring me up now to stay. I know she would rather have me feel bad for her than to feel bad herself, and you weren't created to feel bad."

"You have to see this thing all the way through," said The Chatterbox, joining in.

I tried humming to the muffled sounds of a jingle on TV and continued to press my fingers into my ear as far as they could go. Both the Trollop and Big Fat remained silent as usual, deferring to the more vocal Chatterbox, Perfectionist, and Masculine One.

I deluded myself into thinking that by telling my husband everything going on, I would gain some sort of security and protection from these creatures in my head. I thought that by telling him, I could elicit some validation, but I was feeling just as guilty and confused as ever.

"We are! Face it, deal with it," said the Perfectionist. "Call us what you want to, aspects, figments, insanity walking, whatever. We are! Face it!"

I started to cry. As much as I didn't want to believe the reality that had become my life, I knew the Perfectionist was right. But facing the facts was different than dealing with them, and they were for certain an enormous amount to deal with. For me, facing facts meant reconciling, resigning my fate to them, no matter how strange or unbelievable or absurd. For sure, facing and dealing with the facts, as they existed, were going to be tremendous challenges for me.

Chapter Nineteen

For the next few weeks, Little Me retreated down to the depths of our body's abyss, and I felt abandoned. I could not figure out why Little Me abandoned me to deal with and reconcile her truth. I knew Dr. Townes would rather that I own her truth as mine, but her truth was probably the most difficult of all the questions I needed answers for, and she was unavailable to me. She was so accustomed to retreating for long stretches that her old habits didn't die through therapy. She had retreated for weeks and was not forthcoming with any insights. Since I finally thought I knew who I was in relation to the group, and more or less understood my place, I could probably reconcile my feelings eventually. I just could not figure out why she chose to reveal everything she originally thought best to conceal from me for so long, only to retreat from me when I had so many questions that only she could answer.

I continued to struggle to keep up appearances on the job, and coworkers were noticing that I wasn't nearly as bubbly as usual. I couldn't even hide my mood swings from Marissa, who wasn't buying my excuses about menopause. When I declined her offer for our customary "lilac cutting" sojourn, she was convinced something was desperately wrong with me. After all, I was the one who had turned a chance opportunity to cut some lilacs from the yard of a homeowner not far from where we worked into a yearly rite of spring.

She placed some of the freshly cut lilacs on my desk. "Come on, now, we're friends." I lay my head on my desk.

She pleaded, "You know you can talk to me. There's nothing that you can't tell me."

I started to cry and began to tell her all about my condition. “I’m confounded,” I sobbed. I told her how hard it was to keep up appearances at home and at work, how my moods were swinging wildly back and forth, and that there were others in my head. I told her that the others were relentless in their arguments. “I think Victor will end up leaving me. It’s even affecting my job! I’m so sorry I started this mess,” I cried.

Marissa was stunned. She stared at me with her mouth wide open but speechless. I searched her eyes for something, any emotion, but she was simply too stunned by what she heard. She reached for her telephone and flipped it open to speak. “Yes, I’ll be right there, no problem,” she said, as she turned and quickly walked out of my office.

Sick and Tired sighed and whispered sarcastically, “Phone must have been on vibrate. Now *everybody* will know, you know.”

I spent the rest of the day in my office, with only the light from the blinds coming through. It was cloudy outside and looked as if it would rain. I canceled my session, went home, and crawled into bed.

Week Forty

The Perfectionist dressed me in a beautiful green silk twin-set and navy blue slacks. Big Fat prepared a sumptuous meal of French toast and turkey bacon for me. Time seemed to fly as I picked through the meal, thinking about Little Me and myself.

“Your answer is glaring at you. You went into therapy and created this mess,” said the Masculine One. “I said this was a bad idea from the beginning.”

I ignored the Masculine One’s assessment. It didn’t matter to me if she was right or wrong anymore. The therapy appointment was in two hours, the Masculine One had to drive, and I didn’t intend to engage her in another argument over whose fault it was.

The violent spring snowstorm from the night before left thick sheets of ice and slush on the highway, making the trip slow and arduous to navigate, especially around the curvy, winding road leading to the therapist's office. There was plenty to discuss with Townes, and I hoped we would all get to the Safe Room; we hadn't been there for a while. I pulled up into a snow bank on the farthest side of the lot. Although there weren't many cars parked, both the Perfectionist and the Masculine One weren't taking any chances on getting clipped by a car negotiating its way in or out of the lot. "No dings," insisted the Perfectionist.

This was our first visit since the holidays. My visits had become increasingly sporadic, and I couldn't help feeling anxious and nervous about returning to the Safe Room under my new circumstances. I was used to taking about eight hundred milligrams of ibuprofen for my skull aches and was resigned to at least a dull ache if Little Me decided to show up. Still, I made sure I took some in anticipation of the session, just in case she was summoned outside of the Safe Room instead.

When Dr. Townes opened his office door, his eyes twinkled, and he smiled. I slowly walked into his office, throwing my pocketbook down and flopping onto the couch with a thud. The contents of the pocketbook spilled onto the floor, and I waived away the minor mess, much to the chagrin of the Perfectionist, who wanted to pick it all up and put it all back neatly.

"How was your holiday?" Townes asked, still smiling.

"It was what it was. My husband and my kids were all there. My grandkids were there. Big Fat cooked a wonderful meal, as she always does during the holidays. She made eighteen sweet potato pies this time, and three cakes; two yellow and one devil's food with cream cheese icing. She didn't make the icing though. It was ready-made. My mother was there." I reached down to grab the journals, which had fallen out of the pocketbook onto the floor. "There is a lot in there; should keep you pretty busy."

Dr. Townes looked up over his glasses. "I would like to speak with Little Me now, if you don't mind."

Little Me emerged suddenly, jerking my head and causing it to fall so that my chin rested on my breasts. Little Me moved forward, quickly rising past me, pushing me slightly but not harshly. The ibuprofen hadn't kicked in yet, and my skull began to feel heavy and ached. Then she jumped up from the couch, excited to brimming, almost manic, like milk in a pot left on the stove on a high flame. "I'm here, Doctor," she informed the therapist.

"Little Me, that's good! A really good thing," he said. "Were you able to form some sort of consensus?" he asked.

"No, Doctor," Little Me began. "I honestly don't know what to do now. Some are blaming the Gatekeeper for everything, and she blames me. It's all very troubling. I just expected to remain the way I was during these sessions. I didn't expect you would want me to be in front all the time. Sometimes I want to be in front, and sometimes I don't. I'm having difficulty remaining in front for long periods of time."

Dr. Townes looked somewhat disappointed but didn't seem to want to investigate her feelings outside the Safe Room. "Well, now, let's go into the Safe Room." He turned down the lamp on the table near his chair; not dark, just the usual quiet sort of dim, and then began to speak calmly, "Look to the right, and you see your tree; the leaves are large and still green. The flowers you planted are blooming in the colors that you love, the purples, blues, pinks and yellows. You walk up the stairs; they have been repaired and painted for you."

I felt myself being drawn into the Safe Room, but somehow, something was different. I saw where the steps had been repaired in the front of the house, and noticed the flowers, but decided to change the yellow ones to orange, and then grabbed a few to put into the vase in the center of the foyer. When I got to the foyer, I noticed a fresh bunch of violets already in the vase, white ones, and I liked those so I left them alone. I entered my Safe Room and looked into the large body-length mirror I had placed between the two walls on the left side of the room, where a door had been. I placed the flowers I'd picked into a tall vase on the big round table in the center of the room.

"What are you doing?" Dr. Townes asked.

"Who?" I asked.

"What are you wearing?" he asked.

"I'm wearing what I wore to see you today," I responded.

"Where is Little Me?" he asked.

Little Me looked all grown up and was staring at herself in the mirror as well. We looked almost like twins, except she didn't appear quite as old as I.

"I'm here," she said.

"That's good!" he responded. "This is a good thing. I would like you to ask Sick and Tired to join you both."

Sick and Tired was already watching through the glass of the French door panels, as though she knew beforehand she was going to be summoned. She walked slowly into the Safe Room and took a seat on the comfy couch, which appeared in front of the fireplace. I didn't know which direction Townes was planning to take and wondered why he hadn't requested the others to join us. I had questions for Little Me, but Townes didn't seem interested in me at all; apparently, he was more interested in Sick and Tired. *Perhaps there are no more repressed memories for me to discover*, I thought. It was painfully apparent that the Safe Room was actually for Little Me, and not me, and I felt peculiar in that room now, as one of her fragments.

Obviously unaware of my feelings and seemingly uninterested, Townes began the session as though nothing had changed. But everything had changed. It was all about Little Me and *her* recovery, and I was insignificant, now, or so it seemed. I envied the attention she was getting and felt extremely at odds with my position relative to everyone else. At least they knew about each other. I began to feel extremely alone, and wondered how I would reconcile the feelings of worthlessness I felt.

What difference does it make for me to continue to find out all the sordid details of this life, if at the very least, I know the most important thing about myself by now? Besides, it was my purpose, my job, so to speak, not to know, I thought. I was angry now and interrupted Dr. Townes. "Why is it so important, now that I know who I am, that I have to know anything else?" I screamed.

He explained that part of Little Me's problem in the first place was the fact that events were repressed, "From an important aspect of herself," he said, namely me, apparently, and that now that the repressions were being opened up, it would allow Little Me to move forward toward healing.

Then Dr. Townes changed the focus quickly from me and my questions back to Sick and Tired, who appeared to be the real focus of the day's session. He asked, "Sick and Tired, I'd like you to move through your existence. When exactly did you first feel your existence?" I walked over to the big bow window on the right of the fireplace, sat on the settee and sulked, much like Little Me would have done if pushed aside.

Sick and Tired began, "Oh, I've been around from the beginning, I suspect. I existed, but maybe just not brought out until things got to a point where Little Me needed me to be in front. In terms of my own life though, you already know that it wasn't any crystal stair, that's for sure, but I wouldn't say that I had a life that was necessarily noteworthy. My life could be multiplied by the number of average, lackluster ladies in any town, USA, or certainly any city, and the product would be as so many grains of sand on a beach. I guess the fact that my life is so typical is probably what gives it the significance that begs an opportunity to be heard. You know what I mean?" Sick and Tired let out a long, dry sigh. "That's why I want to thank the Gatekeeper for starting this whole thing, in a way. We needed to know each other, and I don't think that we would have actually met, if she hadn't questioned who she was."

I stood up, shocked and completely undone by what Sick and Tired said. It seemed as though she made a complete about face, which was peculiar indeed, and which only added more to my confusion. She was one of the ones who felt strongest against continuing therapy. She argued with me constantly about the meds and about it being my fault for starting therapy in the first place.

I didn't know whether this reversal of attitude was fortunate for any honest purpose, and was suspicious that it was simply a ploy by her of some kind.

Dr. Townes asked Sick and Tired to continue. "Yeah, when I actually think about it, I have been here all the time, with Little Me. Based on what we learned from The Chatterbox, though, I was definitely brought in after the Gatekeeper, but before the Trollop, the Masculine One, Mushy, and Big Fat. I am not sure if I was before or after the Perfectionist, but I think that I came before her, too. I do think that I was the one most definitely affected by the way we were raised. I wanted to kill myself pretty early on, about age seven or eight, I think." Dr. Townes acknowledged that Sick and Tired was doing very well. Sick and Tired sat up a bit straighter on the couch. Oddly, it appeared that she was actually enjoying her time to be heard.

"Anyway, I came out in front from time to time, but spent most of my time out in front when I was in my twenties, thirties, and a little in my forties. I think the seventies and eighties were the times I was out in front mostly, though, because of the drugs. Langston's poem was all about me, during that time, that's for certain."

Sounding somewhat concerned, Townes asked, "Drugs? What kind of drugs?"

Sick and Tired looked around the room and locked eyes with Little Me. Little Me was visibly nervous, probably because of what she thought Sick and Tired would say, and what I would hear next. She turned away from Sick and Tired, and then ran behind one of the couches to hide. I was hoping that whatever was going to be said about drugs, it wouldn't be as dreadful as all the other revelations I had seen and heard already, and was determined not to be shaken by any of it.

After Little Me disappeared behind the couch, Sick and Tired said rather matter-of-factly, "Oh, marijuana first, at about eighteen, then cocaine. One time I even made a mistake and snorted heroin, thinking it was some sort of brown cocaine."

Of course! Absolutely makes sense! I thought. *With everything else she kept from me, it is completely plausible that the drug stuff would be equally as brutal!* Although I tried to keep a lid on my anger, I was beset with it. In disgust, I shook my head at Little Me, who was still hiding behind the couch.

The Chatterbox sneaked into the room, excited to interject. “That’s a wild story! Do we have time to hear it?”

We didn’t. The angels came into the room and stood at the four corners.

"The doors we open and close each day decide the lives we live."

—Flora Whitmore

Chapter Twenty

Exhausted, but peculiarly at ease, considering what I'd heard, I acknowledged my appointment for the next visit and left his office. On the way home I stopped at the store to get some more journals, and then rushed to see if Sick and Tired would want to write. After cooking some dinner for Victor, I went upstairs to journal.

"Let's see. The first time I snorted cocaine," Sick and Tired began as I wrote. "I can't remember. But I do remember the first joint I smoked. It was with Snake. Mushy was around by then, and I believe it was she who was thoroughly infatuated by him, but that's beside the point. We were at his house, and I had been sitting there waiting for his cousin, Gilbert, to show up since Snake's house was the place where us kids congregated. As always, Gilbert was the absentee boyfriend, even though we had been together for about a year by that time. I told the therapist I was eighteen, but I was actually sixteen by these calculations. I was sitting down on the couch in Snake's living room listening to music, and Snake came midway down the stairway holding a joint. He motioned for me to join him upstairs to smoke it. I eagerly followed him to his mother's bedroom, and he taught me how.

"Not that I was any sort of angel, I was already getting drunk on cheap wine at parties on a pretty regular basis. I started that at fifteen, but the hard stuff, the really hard drugs, all that came later, when I was about nineteen."

I cracked the cramp out of my fingers and continued to write. "I recall that Gilbert and I were at a party thrown by one of Snake's brothers who fancied himself a drug kingpin in the city, but I always suspected he was his own best fan. I remember how old I was by then, because most of the men at the party thought I was very attractive, calling me 'young meat,' when I mentioned to Snake's brother that I was nineteen. It's just a good damn thing that the Trollop wasn't close to the surface then. She didn't come out at all when we were with Gilbert, and Mushy remained loyal to him for a long time, poor thing. That's why I spent more time with Mushy than just about anybody else."

Sick and Tired paused, sighed, and continued. "Anyway, I remember immediately noticing that there was no furniture in the front room, save for a long glass dining table and about eight chairs positioned around it in the corner near the beginning of the hallway to the bedrooms. I walked into one of the bedrooms where I saw a large punch bowl filled with what I thought was cocaine. People were scooping up the brown powder and taking it away to the bathroom, or snorting it in the room. When I asked what it was, I was told that it was brown coke from Mexico. 'Mexican Brown' they called it, so I snorted it, and snorted it and snorted it. After a short while, as I sat at the dining table in the front room, I felt sleepy, very sleepy, so groggy that I could barely keep my head up from the table. Gilbert nudged me hard in my side; apparently, I had fallen asleep. I was slobbering and found it extremely difficult to bring my head up from the table. I was so confused. Cocaine never made me feel sleepy or disoriented, but I was both. Gilbert was getting angry with me. He kept saying, 'Stop noddin' out!' Finally, I got up from the table and found a small area on the floor in a corner between two people having a drunken discussion, and disappeared into a nod that I didn't recover from until I found myself at Gilbert's house in his sister's bed the next afternoon. That was when I found out that I had ingested heroin. That was the first and last time for that."

"So much for being the Gatekeeper," I said, mortified. I would never have condoned snorting anything, and I was angry that Sick and Tired was allowed to have such a strong influence at that time. *Obviously, I had to have been overruled to let her get away with snorting heroin*, I thought.

Suddenly, Sick and Tired stopped speaking when a voice I didn't recognize filled my head.

"Oh, God, how I really loved Snake. I adored him. He was so smart, and so pretty. He died much too young, before I could make him see his own worth. I could have changed him, I know it." It was Mushy. We hadn't heard very much from her since therapy began.

The Masculine One rose quickly to the surface and retorted, "Oh, come the hell off it, Mushy! You see worth in a rock! He was a loser who died from a heroin overdose on his mother's birthday, on Christmas Day! What is with you and Sick and Tired? Snake would have been worse than Gilbert, and living with Gilbert was like living in Hell itself! Goddammit, it never failed, whenever the three of you overruled me, everybody suffered! I was the one who tried to keep the more levelheaded among us, like the Perfectionist or myself, in front. No doubt I might even have considered the Gatekeeper for the front if I knew more about her before."

I must admit that I wasn't shocked listening to the Masculine One arguing with Mushy. I was positive that more times than not, some bizarre fusing or outlandish alliances took place over the years with these mental misfits living in this body. Up until now, though, Mushy wasn't contributing anything, so I figured she finally wanted to chime in just because Sick and Tired wrote about Snake, and it pushed her love button. I remembered that the Masculine One was perpetually annoyed with Sick and Tired, but I forgot that she wasn't very happy about Mushy, either. That would explain why she became incensed once again. Since the therapist wanted everyone to contribute, I did not object when Mushy jumped to the surface and began to write.

"Where to begin, except at the beginning. It was 1968, and I was fifteen years old. Martin Luther King had died that year, and it was also the year I met Gilbert. I met him through one of the girls I still hung around with from junior high. She and I fancied us best friends. Her nickname was Sloody. Sloody was in love with Snake, even though he was going with our mutual friend Tweeter, but then, Sloody was a slut, after all.

"We went to a party one Saturday night. Partying was customary for the two of us; we partied a great deal. Sloody must have known that Snake would be at the party. When we got there, I started drinking almost immediately. There were always both wine and beer at the parties we went to, although I didn't drink the beer. I didn't like beer. After a while, a group of boys strolled into the party, dressed really sharp, and most were very, very cute. All the girls were fawning all over them, and I believe some actually swooned. I heard through the crowd of onlookers that it was the 'World Dance Society,' and kept hearing names like Snake and T-B. I wiggled through some of the crowd to see so If I could place the faces with the names. Then I saw Snake. He was absolutely beautiful, with deep, dark eyes, the flaming kind that seemed to pierce through me, but in a good way; a good burn. I was caught up. He was seated on a stool and he was staring at me in much the same way that I stared at him, and I was instantly in love."

"Bullshit!" yelled the Masculine One. "You were drunk off that cheap dollar wine! You shouldn't have been drinking at fifteen years old, anyway!" I had to agree with the Masculine One. Mushy, however, ignored the Masculine One, admitted to being drunk, and then continued to write.

"After a while, though, I got so drunk I was cross-eyed. I couldn't do anything about what I was feeling about Snake anyway, since Tweeter and Sloody were all over him. Besides, I didn't believe in messing around with a friend's boyfriend like Sloody did. She was the slut, not me. After a while, when some of the girls started kissing T-B, who was sitting in a chair near the front door, the Trollop stepped up to join them, and I just hung close to her. He was no Snake, but he was cute with his big lips, in a tall, boney, lanky sort of way. He kissed well, or I thought he did at the time. Turned out that he was Snake's cousin, Gilbert," she chuckled. "What a way to meet the one who I eventually married and bore two wonderful children for! How about that, met at fifteen, married at twenty-one—"

The Masculine One could hear no more and broke in, jumping in front of Mushy, and at once, my head began to pound. "Yeah, and divorced at twenty-eight! You were fifteen years old and drunk, you idiot! When you got drunk, the only ones who would even want to be around you were that slut, the Trollop, or Big Fat or Sick and Tired. You are always just too fuckin' friendly, which means anybody could walk all over your stupid ass. You all drank, Big Fat ate us into oblivion, the Trollop gave us Trichomonas, and Sick and Tired did drugs. I hated that Little Me only allowed me to watch from the background while you all made a complete mess of our life! And I can't believe that now you're trying to glamorize it, as though we all had a great time with Lucifer himself! Gilbert fought you and Sick and Tired most of the time, stole from you all the time, and belittled Big Fat, which only made Sick and Tired all the sicker and tired of being sick and tired. The Trollop even stopped coming out, and it's just a good damn thing that she didn't because Gilbert would have had more reason to beat us up."

The Masculine One was fuming. "I wasn't so worried about you as I was about Little Me. I could have killed Gilbert at any time, but then Little Me would have suffered. We would all have gone to prison or worse, and why, because of stupidity." The Masculine One was incensed and I could feel her stomping and fuming around inside my head. "You all could probably have cared less about being in prison, anyway. Why, there'd be food, plenty to be sick and tired about, and even relationships. At least there'd be some sort of screwing, and the Trollop would have adjusted, I'm sure. But, my job was and remains to be to protect Little Me, even if it meant keeping that bastard alive, and staying in the background."

Mushy was embarrassed. She stopped writing and stepped so far back that she could barely be felt. Clearly, the Masculine One had disrupted her once too often. I closed the journal to reflect. Thanks to Little Me, I only had vague recollections, if any, about much of what the Masculine One said. As the Gatekeeper, I knew I had to have existed then, at least during most of the time. Perhaps I was there with Sick and Tired and the others during that time, all the while, as Little Me said, oblivious, somehow walking through this life with these others, as the "good face" in place of the battered, drunk, drugged, diseased, or obese faces. *How utterly insane*! I thought.

"You behave as though we had a choice!" Mushy lashed back uncharacteristically at the Masculine One, "We didn't have a choice! You weren't the only one protecting Little Me. We protected Little Me, too. She wasn't getting beat up. That was me. She wasn't getting fat. That was Big Fat."

Sick and Tired weighed in. "She wasn't taking drugs! That was me!" Sick and Tired and Mushy were unnerved by the Masculine One's seemingly holier than thou attitude. "What you are forgetting is that we united briefly in 1983.

While the Gatekeeper and the Perfectionist kept the kids safe and found the good job with the law firm, we all pulled away from Gilbert, including you. The Perfectionist was able to get us a divorce, with a great deal of help from The Chatterbox, who talked our way into getting it done for free."

All of the explanations did nothing to keep the Masculine One from fuming, since not much kept her from fuming except the meds, which I hadn't taken yet. I could feel that Mushy was embarrassed by what the Masculine One said to her, and chills were running up and down our collective spine. My head ached as though they were fist fighting in there, and I felt especially sad, since, according to Townes, we were all in this mess together. Mushy was decidedly against continuing to write as long as the Masculine One was nearby. I had to agree, since I was exhausted from the exercise, and if I was ever going to get some sleep, things would have to quiet down considerably. I managed, though, after some coaxing, to get Mushy to agree to talk in the Safe Room, where boundaries could be placed, and it would be more difficult for the Masculine One to disrupt.

Chapter Twenty-One

Week Fifty

Weeks of aimless stares, countless dropped calls, and indiscrete cancellations for lunch later, the realization I'd told Marissa too much was all the more evident when I arrived at work. She was a stranger, and not the person who, over the years, I'd felt so comfortable confiding in. I felt so betrayed by her. She gave me confidence to tell her about my condition and myself because she said that nothing I could tell her would shock her. Apparently, there was, and it was that she was the friend and coworker of a lunatic.

At our weekly staff meeting, I kept my head down, staring at the reflections of other staffers and anything visible from the glass conference tabletop. I raised my eyes and met Marissa's, who quickly turned away. I was convinced I was watching the death of my friendship and would have to mourn it in much the same way that I had to mourn the life I knew I would never have again, now that I was just a piece of Little Me.

I allowed Sick and Tired to move into the front position. I just couldn't keep up. I knew too much, and I couldn't find the time before it all began anymore. Before was in the distant past now, and there was no going back there, for sure.

When I arrived for my session, Dr. Townes mentioned that he had finally completed most of the volumes of journal entries I'd handed him the during the many weeks earlier.

His demeanor appeared much more anxious, and he didn't try to hide his concern. "You were so hurt, and it made me feel extremely sad for you," he said. He placed his hand on my shoulder. "I won't belabor any of the hurtful points in the journals. Just know that those things are gone, and you never have to worry about them coming back."

I told him once again that he was talking to me and not Little Me.

He said, "One day I will be, and you will be happy about it."

I shuddered to think of the possibility and shrugged off his comment.

Although my intention was to go into the Safe Room, Dr. Townes wanted to talk to Little Me from outside, and I wasn't prepared for Little Me to emerge. "I would like to speak to Little Me today. Would you bring her out?" he asked. I didn't really want to oblige him, since I knew I would get a horrible ache in my skull, because I hadn't taken any ibuprofen before the visit.

Suddenly, I began to feel Little Me struggling to come out to the front. My head got heavy again as Little Me made her way toward the surface. "I'm here," she said, a little out of breath.

Dr. Townes smiled and said, "You are such a wonderful person. You are the best, absolutely the best."

I felt myself cringe. How I hated him so much when he said that. I wouldn't have cared if the Masculine One erupted on him, if she spewed every ounce of the fiery, molten profanity boiling inside me at that moment. All he cared about was Little Me.

Little Me thanked him but seemed unenthusiastic. Perhaps my feeling about him blended into hers—a thought that made me smile, but just a bit.

He began the session. "How old are you today?"

"I'm ageless, you know that," she said.

Dr. Townes seemed taken aback by her statement. "That was a rather odd response to my question, for someone so young, Little Me. Could you explain that response for me?"

Her statement also confused me, but I could do nothing but sit in the background while she unfolded in front of me, hoping Dr. Townes would ask the right questions.

"Well," she began, "that means nothing, and it means everything. Right now, I'm grown Little Me. Today I'm grown."

Dr. Townes drew in closer to Little Me and began to write on his notepad, listening intently.

Little Me sighed and said, "Thing is, though, it would be nice if I could stay in front all of the time as myself the way I am now, and the way I am dressed today, but I can't. I can't because the reality is that the Perfectionist dressed me today. I had a rough day at the office today, so the Masculine One was out for most of it, handling the Albatross for me. Most of the time, I don't even really want to come out at all," she admitted.

Little Me abruptly began to shift from an adult to a child, curling her legs on the couch. "It's pretty scary out there. I am afraid most times, so I try to stay back. Then I am forced to come out when I don't want to, now that the Gatekeeper is mad at me. Nobody wants to help me anymore, but they want to do what they want." Little Me shifted back into an adult again. "The only reason why I haven't brought up Sick and Tired is because of the meds, and I am not whoring around because the Trollop only comes out when I'm not married, thank God."

The shifting back and forth was making me nervous. Dr. Townes listened intently as Little Me continued. "You see, Doctor, because of the choices I made from the beginning of the time that I knew choices existed, these ladies have tried to shield me and protect me by acting out the choices I made in the first place. I have to admit I was surprised that the Gatekeeper hated me now for what happened when I was much younger. But that only means that I hated myself. I know that."

Dr. Townes appeared troubled by the apparent contradictions in Little Me's explanations. "Little Me, you have progressed such a great deal from our first visit so many months ago. But choices were certainly *not* what you had as a small child. You *do* understand that, don't you?"

Apparently, he didn't realize that Little Me was shifting back and forth and the little girl had different feelings than the grown up. He raised his brow slightly and looked at Little Me over his glasses. "You said that none of the others want to help you, and that they want to do what they want. You also said that sometimes you really don't want to come out at all. You need to understand that in order for us to move toward your healing, you control the parts of yourself, not the other way around. You will be integrating the others and converging into a whole person, the way you should have been before your trauma. You do understand that you will need to let go of the others as separates then, don't you?"

Little Me shifted back to the little girl. "Oh, I'll *never* let go of them," she cautioned. She shifted quickly back to the adult and sat up straight, looking directly at Townes. "Remember, I didn't ask for this. I need them. They prop me up. At any time, in any place, and for any reason, I can summon one, two, or all of them to handle any situation. We will always be bound together, and if it has to be as separates, then that's just the way it will have to be, period."

Dr. Townes grew visibly troubled by what he was hearing. "That's true, Little Me, but it seems to me you think somehow what they do on your behalf is separate from you. The truth is that what they do undoubtedly affects you, and what you do directly affects them. I'm trying to help you gain control of yourself, and not defer to the others when you think you can't handle something by yourself."

"I know that, and that is not right!" Little Me became annoyed with his explanations. I didn't really like what he was implying either but wasn't able to speak. Certainly, I didn't want to integrate. I didn't even know what that meant. *What's convergence?* I thought. I worried that Little Me might decide to leave abruptly, since she was shifting back and forth so erratically, and that the Masculine One would step in front of her.

Little Me jumped up from the couch, folded her arms around each other, and shouted, "Doctor, I don't think you understand what's really going on with me! This is a waste of time!"

Dr. Townes' eyes were wide and his mouth flung open. He seemed somewhat confused by Little Me's growing agitation but didn't let up on her. "If you or they act out on something contrary to what any or all of you want to do, say, wear, or be, don't you think that the potential results can be risky or even dangerous?"

"I understand all of that, and my life has already been risky. Let me see. According to you, I created the others because of the trauma of being raped by Mr. Peace. I don't even know that for sure. You suggested it one day in the Safe Room and we all bought it. All the other stuff I know about because I lived it. Perhaps I could have let the Gatekeeper in on things sooner, you know, ease her in when she became aware enough to question, but then, I'm no psychiatrist, and my Gatekeeper had her purpose just like the others. She couldn't know things and keep it all together for me at the same time. It would have been impossible." Little Me was angry, and I was confused by her anger. I couldn't understand what she was angry about, unless the thought of integration upset her as much as it did me.

Dr. Townes attempted to calm her down. "Obviously there were behaviors that were risky and dangerous, but you overcame them on your own, Little Me," he said, and pointed out how Little Me managed to raise her children to become well-adjusted adults, despite the trauma and adversity.

In an attempt to get closer to Little Me, I tried to move next to her, but she pushed me back. I tried to ask her why she was angry and was ignored.

Then, just as abruptly, Little Me seemed to calm down, but only a little, apparently still slightly annoyed with the therapist. She pulled off her shoes and put her feet up on the couch, stretching her legs close to the arm at the end.

Dr. Townes leaned back in his chair and took off his glasses to clean them, still watching Little Me, who was noticeably calmer, playing with the teddy bear that always rested on the couch. They sat quietly for a time, as Little Me tossed the teddy bear up and down through the air and he watched intently, tapping lightly on the arms of his chair with his fingers. Then Little Me gently placed the teddy bear back on its bottom, close to her feet, and looked directly at Townes. She found a rubber band on the couch and began to twist it around her finger.

I felt slightly more assured that the Masculine One wouldn't disrupt the session since Little Me was significantly calmer. Townes asked Little Me how old she was.

"I was five, then I was thirty, but now I'm about fifty," she said softly. Then she sighed and whispered, "I have never been in complete control of my life, EVER. The others have evolved to become distinct, purposeful, and useful enough for me to stay away altogether."

Dr. Townes spoke to Little Me, carefully weighing every word before he spoke, not wanting to re-ignite her agitation and anxiety any further. "Eventually, one or more of the others may want to take over. How do you think you would handle it if one wanted complete control?" He waited for Little Me to respond.

An unexpected knock at the door interrupted us.

Dr. Townes excused himself, closing the door behind him. Those of us who were nearest to Little Me began to feel extremely anxious. Little Me was in deep thought and wouldn't respond to anyone who tried to engage her. She did allow us to watch her thoughts in much the same way that I had done many times with the others.

She was back to the late eighties when we were living with the second husband, Milton. The thoughts drifted back to a time when I was pregnant with my third baby, David, and my older two from Gilbert were ten and eight. Sick and Tired wasn't drinking, but she, the Trollop and Mushy were back to smoking cigarettes again. It appeared that the Masculine One, the Perfectionist, and I were holding down the financial obligations. We watched as the Perfectionist put Milton's small paper factory pay into our dresser drawer and as Milton withdrew portions of it, whenever he needed money, until he ran out, coincidentally right around the time when he got paid again, continuing the cycle.

The Perfectionist whispered, "That way, I could guarantee he wouldn't steal from us." Little Me sighed and I felt somewhat sorry for her, which was a tremendous stretch for me, given my feelings. I could feel Sick and Tired trying to rise to the front of Little Me, so we all held her back.

I admonished Sick and Tired, "She's just thinking about a sad time. She isn't asking for you."

Little Me reached inward for our attention, but she already had it, undivided. Then she said, "I knew that my relationship with Milton was over before we got married. I knew he was bad, that he killed his own cousin. That's why The Chatterbox named him the Assassin. He was evil from the beginning, but instead of dropping him like I should have, when I could have, I shoved myself into an unfathomable depth, allowing Sick and Tired and Mushy to deal with my life with him." She continued talking about Milton, focusing on the time when Milton punched Sick and Tired and Mushy in the head repeatedly and bit them in the back one day while they breast-fed baby David.

The Masculine One recalled the visions for me. "He was coming home from getting high with his friends, and one of them called the house to let Sick and Tired know that he was cheating. She got upset and so did I. When he got to the bedroom, Mushy was breast-feeding the baby, and I announced that we were leaving as soon as the baby got a little older. He didn't even seem to get angry, so I went back down into the background, where I was resting. Up until then, he hadn't been violent, so I had no reason to believe he would start. Even so, very unpredictably, he walked around to the back of the chair and began to pummel their head and then bit them on the back. By the time I got back up to the front, they were already pleading with him to stop, and I thought it was better for all if I didn't do anything, especially with the baby still in their arms."

Dr. Townes returned with a cup of coffee for Little Me, and a cup of tea for himself, and then excused himself again, explaining that he had another emergency call. Little Me was sulking as a feeling of fear washed over me. *Convergence means we will all melt into one.* I thought. *I will lose myself for sure, maybe even die.* The others were getting restless and moving around, jockeying for positions closer to Little Me, no doubt feeling the way I was about the depressing thoughts swirling around us. I began to feel suspicious of Little Me. She was thinking that we were at the root of her problems. I thought her feelings were outlandish at least, and offensive at best. I was afraid she was beginning to buy what Dr. Townes said about us eventually leaving her. She was considering the prospect of converging and integrating. To me, that notion was obscene. Without a doubt, in my view, I wasn't the reason she needed therapy. *I* was the one *she* had kept things from. If anything, it was *her* insanity that had brought us to where we were now.

Little Me blew into her Styrofoam cup filled with hot, black coffee, just the way she and the Perfectionist liked to drink it. She took a small sip, slightly burning her tongue.

Dr. Townes finally returned and sat in his chair.

"Can I tell you something?" asked Little Me.

"Absolutely," he said, sitting up in his chair and listening intently.

"I really cared for Milton and he really hurt me. As a result, I gave Mushy and Sick and Tired entirely too much control during that time. At first, I thought that using the Trollop was the best way to get close, but it was Mushy who took my feelings completely overboard and Sick and Tired who actually got me into the drug trouble. Between the two of them, they made my life a disaster.

Anyway, I need to tell you about the first time I saw Milton freebase cocaine, okay, because that was major."

Dr. Townes appeared a bit surprised but didn't interrupt.

"Milton always loved people around him and loved to entertain. One night, he invited his friend, Brother Earl, to the house to watch the game. Of course, Brother Earl brought their friend, Candy Baby, and some other woman with him." Little Me sighed, rolled her eyes and continued. "Anyway, Milton always had company over the house. On this particular night, they all sat in the living room, fidgeting, and looking back and forth at each other; all wondering when something that was supposed to happen was going to happen. Whatever was supposed to happen was certainly *not* going to happen as long as I was downstairs with them. That was for sure. Finally, Milton told me to go to bed, since 'you need your rest.' I resisted leaving for a while, but the uneasiness in the room suggested that it would be better for me to remove myself. When I got upstairs, the Masculine One slammed Mushy for being so accommodating and allowing them to take over the house."

Little Me pulled her shoulders back defiantly. "After all, whose house was it anyway? Sometimes I wonder if Milton actually thought that I didn't know anything about what he was doing. At any rate, he thought he was keeping me in the dark about it, but I knew they were doing drugs. I knew it was cocaine, and I knew they were smoking it. I had just never seen it done before. I began to imagine freebasing as some sort of a group sport or something. And if you can believe this, I was jealous that I was pregnant and couldn't do it with them. I actually thought they were having 'all the fun.' So I decided I had to go downstairs to see it for myself. All I needed was an excuse and Big Fat gave it to me. I was going downstairs to get some juice. I was thirsty. That was it. I was thirsty. He couldn't get an attitude about me being thirsty.

"So I went downstairs and walked into the kitchen in just enough time to see Milton holding the crack pipe to his lips while Brother Earl held the lit matches. That was the first time I saw it being done."

Dr. Townes said, "They were in the kitchen? Freebasing cocaine?"

"Yes," said Little Me. "And I was jealous. I was jealous because I was pregnant and couldn't do it with them. I believed those women were closer to my husband than I was, and thought they were closer because they were doing it together, you know, the group sport of it all."

Dr. Townes eased back into his chair, and grabbed his glasses from his eyes, wiping the water with his forearm that had collected on his brow. He asked, "Little Me, where were your children during all this?"

Little Me thought for a while, reaching inside for the others to get answers but no one offered, not even The Chatterbox. "I suppose they were asleep by that time. I'm not sure. Perhaps the Gatekeeper or the Perfectionist put them to bed for me. I do know they weren't around when it happened. After it happened, I just took my juice, walked back upstairs, and didn't come down again."

Little Me took her feet off the couch and sat upright. She grabbed her shoes by their sling backs as she checked out the clock on the end table. The time had flown again.

"We should stop," Dr. Townes said. "But I think we need time to discuss this further. I'd like to see you again this week."

Little Me nodded and Dr. Townes gave her an appointment for Friday. "Doctor, that's this Friday?" she asked. He nodded, and Little Me assured him she would see him Friday, then left his office.

Still in front when she got into the car, Little Me was hard pressed to enlist anyone to take the wheel for the drive home. I didn't really like to drive anymore, so I wasn't offering, deferring most times to the Masculine One, but since she was being as pigheaded as Little Me, we sat in the parking lot, watching all the other cars as one by one they left. After over an hour of wrangling back and forth, I finally succeeded in convincing a very reluctant Masculine One into putting the keys in the ignition and driving us home.

Little Me struggled to stay in front every day, a fact which caused me a great deal of angst, since I knew from the therapy sessions that she really didn't want to be there. As a matter of fact, we were all struggling to maintain our own positions and identities. The others were beginning to believe Little Me was making a play for convergence and integration at our expense. It seemed that although the Perfectionist had become accustomed to handling wardrobe, Little Me would try to do it herself. Big Fat handled cooking and pleasure eating, but Little Me stopped cooking altogether and was eating less and less. Little Me was keeping us all at bay, not allowing us to perform the functions that we all had been used to performing. We all knew Little Me was more accustomed to staying in the background, opting to let us control her, but she was questioning us now, as though we were her problem to solve. She seemed angrier with us, and me in particular, when I had all the right in the world to loath her. We weren't her problem. We were the ones who kept her alive. She used to understand that. Sometimes I felt like I was losing the very ground that I'd worked so hard to stand on during all these months of therapy.

If perplexity over the way she felt about us and our eventual fate wasn't enough, at the same time, Little Me still summoned us, which only confused us more. At times which we found were unnecessary at best, and ridiculous at worst, she would thrust one or more of us to the surface to deal with something we weren't even created to deal with. It was obvious that she didn't know what she wanted to do with herself, or us, which was a fact that we were all finding exceedingly difficult not to rebel against.

By Thursday, the day before the next scheduled therapy session, Little Me was practically begging us to help her in her day to day activities, something we would have done without hesitation before.

"Why should I even bother to go up front anymore?" I asked Little Me, who was beckoning for me to replace her at work. "We have to go to therapy tomorrow, and I'll have to be aware all afternoon. I really need to relax, to rest up." Little Me continued to plead with me until I reluctantly moved to the front to handle our day, not wishing to engage Sick and Tired, who appeared more than willing to go in my place if asked. By Friday, Little Me could no longer be felt among us, having retreated yet again.

When we drove into the parking lot of the therapist's office, Mushy came up just close enough to the surface to admire the summer flowers that had begun to bloom in the area, seemingly oblivious to the fact that we couldn't feel Little Me anymore. "Look at all the beautiful flowers! They're everywhere!" Mushy gushed.

Mushy, Little Me, and I loved the summer season almost as much as we loved spring. Mushy and I paused in front of the building, taking in the fragrance from all the beautiful flowers that bloomed on the side of the wall between the windows. At first, I thought for sure Little Me would at least come to the surface to look at them, but she had retreated too deeply.

Still bubbling and gushing over the flowers, Mushy announced, "If we ever go back into the Safe Room, I'm going to put some lilacs right in front of the large bow windows!"

Dr. Townes was on time for our visit. In fact, he was waiting at the front door when I arrived. He explained that the alarm system was down again. I sat down on the couch and took off my shoes. They weren't very comfortable and not particularly fashionable, but then, the Perfectionist didn't want to pick out what to wear. They were not cooperating with Little Me and were not offering any assistance to me either. They were still angry with me for bringing everybody out into the open.

Dr. Townes sat in his chair, preparing his notes and setting up his note pad. He began by asking for Little Me.

"Doctor, it's me, the Gatekeeper," I said. I finally had a name and was slightly reconciled as to my purpose, but it was still a small consolation by now. The fact was Little Me was still away, with no prospect of returning. "Little Me retreated somewhere on Thursday, saying she needed to rest, but only for a day I thought. The others were distressed by the last session and the way she made us feel, so we didn't cooperate very much with her. But who can blame us?"

The Masculine One interrupted, pushing me to the back. "One minute she wants us to stay with her and do the work of living for her, and then the next minute, she wants to listen to your shit and kill us off." I didn't apologize for the Masculine One; I had to admit I approved of everything she said this time.

"Well," Townes said, appearing disappointed but not thwarted, "let's go into the Safe Room. She may come there and it will certainly be easier on your head." He turned down the lights to their customary dusky dim while I positioned myself on the couch, placing the teddy bear under my head like a pillow.

As soon as I got into the Safe Room, Mushy headed toward one of the large bow windows. "Ah," she said, "there they are!" referring to the fully bloomed lilacs that filled the outside of both windows.

"Where are you?" Dr. Townes asked.

"In the Safe Room with Mushy."

He requested the others, and they obliged, one by one, until all were present; all except for Little Me.

"She's not here," I said, concerned because I still couldn't feel her. As though sensing my concern, Dr. Townes became the stern disciplinarian much the same way he did whenever he thought Little Me was being obstinate. Then, with a noticeable lack of enthusiasm, Little Me entered the Safe Room, dressed the way I was dressed but appearing about twenty years younger than me.

"I really don't want to be here," she sniped. "Not for nothing, I would have eventually come up in the doctor's office without coming into the Safe Room, but no one gave me enough time to do it. I was getting there," she said, rolling her eyes at me.

"Are you there, Little Me? What do you have on today?" Dr. Townes asked, since lately her age fluctuated frequently. Little Me would not answer. I explained that Little Me was wearing the same thing I wore when I arrived for the session, and that we looked identical today, except for our ages. Townes asked Little Me if she would assist in the Safe Room.

She decided to cooperate, all the while still rolling her eyes at anyone whose eyes met hers in the room. She pushed one of the chairs in the room as far away from the rest of us as she could without leaving the room altogether, and announced, "Doctor, I need to tell you some things."

She began, "You know, I bet when Mushy first found out that Milton was available, that's when I allowed myself to relinquish my control to both the Trollop and Mushy too easily. Of course, then the Trollop went out hunting for him to screw him. By the time my youngest was born, Mushy was already married and getting beat up by Milton. Then to make matters worse, the Trollop stepped back, abandoning Mushy, I suppose because of her rule concerning only coming out when I'm single. When the Trollop left, then Sick and Tired moved in with Mushy. Mushy unrealistically believed in a love that was unrequited, causing a profound depression to set in."

Little Me was talking ridiculously, as if she was having one of the epiphanies that I was so used to having. *Profound? Unrequited? Where were these words coming from?* I wondered. Trepidation gripped me as I listened to Little Me ramble on. I could see the Masculine One beginning to heat up. The Perfectionist began pacing back and forth from the fireplace to where she had been originally sitting. We all could taste the antagonistic flavor of gruel, which she fed the therapist at our expense. Big Fat and the others sat stunned, listening but not reacting for fear of appearing to take sides.

Dr. Townes stopped Little Me. "You seem to be drawing conclusions about the others concerning your relationship with Milton. Are you saying you entered a profound depression?"

"No!" Little Me shouted, suddenly annoyed that the therapist apparently misunderstood her. "Of course it was Sick and Tired who got severely depressed. After my youngest was about a year old, Sick and Tired and Mushy began to freebase crack cocaine with Milton."

Little Me glared at Sick and Tired and Mushy. "Mushy did it because she thought that doing so would draw her closer to Milton, and because she figured Milton couldn't possibly be the devil that he was. Sick and Tired did it because she was miserable, and if there was anything she could do to add to it, she would. The drugs served her purpose. She just kept doing it because of how it made her feel." Sick and Tired and Mushy were shocked by what Little Me said, since she was apparently drawing more conclusions for them.

In a flash, Little Me stood up before everyone in the room and announced, "Even now I shudder to think that I could either be dead or a raving two dollar crack head prostitute by now. She sat back down, wiping a small amount of perspiration from her brow with her forearm.

For just an instant, my mind felt like an old vinyl record being scratched across its face by the needle. Had I missed something in her ranting? I had to try to piece together the portions that I heard. *Raving, two dollar crack head prostitute?* This revelation should have been more than I could take in, but I was oddly secure in the knowledge of what I was sure would come out of her mouth next.

Evidently, Townes wasn't quite as secure. "Crack?" he asked, apparently concerned that Little Me could have been an addict. I heard the sound of pages flipping rapidly. I could only imagine him thumbing hurriedly through his papers to find some prior, forgotten reference to crack.

"I remember you mentioning drug use, but to what extent isn't clear. *You* were freebasing? You're talking about Milton, your second husband. How did you come to know Milton and then marry him in the first place, in just two years after your divorce from Gilbert, and when did you start using crack?"

Dr. Townes flooded Little Me with questions all at once. Little Me heaved a sigh and then looked into the air as though searching through it, like something in the air would tell her how she ever got to this place. "All right, I'll tell you when I first laid eyes on Milton. Then hopefully everything will make sense." I moved in closer to hear, and was relieved that we were in the Safe

Room and that the details of this revelation wouldn't come out at home as a flashback.

Chapter Twenty-Two

"It was in the fifth grade during assembly," She began. "I thought he was cute even back then. During that time, there were only glimpses, fleeting moments where our paths intersected, and he was always smiling; pleasant, full of manners and respect. It wasn't long before I had a crush on him, but so did many other girls. Let me be clear, *I* had a crush on Milton, not Mushy; at least not Mushy right away."

Dr. Townes stopped Little Me. "You knew him a long time, I see. When did you get romantically involved with him?"

Little Me continued as though she hadn't heard his question. "After I broke up with Gilbert briefly in the early seventies, you have to understand that I was having the time of my life. I was entertaining other men, like Reed back then, but I digress. Anyway, I mean, I was going out to parties and having a great time enjoying my freedom. I was twenty years old without a care in the world, or at least that's the way the Gatekeeper kept it for me. One night, I went to a party and ran into our mutual friend, Brother Earl. Of course, I asked how Milton was doing, and of course, he had all of the right answers about him. One night, I invited them to come to my apartment to play pinochle. Milton brought his cousin Phil, and I invited a couple of my girlfriends. We had a great time, drinking, smoking weed, playing cards, and playing drinking games. Once, Milton came over by himself, and we kissed for the first time. After that time, he would come to visit more often by himself. I kept the Trollop away back then, so we never had sex during that time.

"On one particular night, Milton and Phil dropped by to visit. I wasn't involved, or so I thought, so when Reed and his roommate came by, I thought the situation couldn't have been more perfect. After a short while, Milton calmly excused himself, and he and Phil left. After that time, I didn't see Milton again until the mid seventies, not so long after I married Gilbert, had my first child, and was pregnant with my baby girl. We were at a party, and then I saw him. He was with his entourage. He had on a long black camelhair coat. All I know is that I really thought he looked almost presidential as he sauntered in with his group. Much later I would discover that they hid shotguns and rifles inside those long black coats, that they were real gangsters."

Little Me fanned herself, as though just thinking of that time scorched her insides. She was perspiring more and appeared uncomfortable. "Anyway, I giggled with the group of girlfriends I was standing with. I realized at that moment that I still had a crush on him. When he walked over to me, I took the opportunity to ask what he had been doing. I learned that he and Brother Earl, Ice-Pick, his cousin Phil, and a host of others were in the business of selling weed by the pound and evidently had become very successful at it. After that party, I wouldn't see Milton anymore during the seventies, but there were all sorts of stories about him floating around my circle of friends; stories of home invasions, robberies, and murder that swirled around him but failed to touch him."

Dr. Townes stopped Little Me again. "You still haven't told me when you married Milton. Did the Trollop or Mushy cause you to leave Gilbert for Milton?"

"Excuse me," Little Me said, a little embarrassed. "I was too busy reminiscing and forgot where I was." She paused for a moment to wipe the sweat that was building on her face. "No. The Trollop came out after my divorce from Gilbert. After Gilbert, I went far inside and allowed Mushy and the Trollop to carry on for me. I couldn't handle the pain from my marriage and divorce from Gilbert but didn't realize just how bad Mushy and the Trollop would make things after the divorce. In fact, The Trollop was in front by herself for a long while."

Dr. Townes was intrigued. "She was in front and handling your life for a long time by herself?"

The Masculine One broke the silence for the others in the room. "Frankly, I don't think we have enough fucking time to discuss all the other men that she slept with, the damn slut."

Dr. Townes ignored the Masculine One, opting to elicit an answer from Little Me. "Can you elaborate for me, please?"

The Masculine One was infuriated with Little Me for bringing up the other men. "The Trollop is a slut," she said.

The Trollop stood up and shouted, "If I'm a slut, then you're a slut, and we're all sluts! That's a fact! It's been proven; we're all the same, and every man I slept with you did, too!"

Little Me ignored the Masculine One and the Trollop. She was sweating more and more and got up to make sure the large bow windows were opened. She asked for a refreshing breeze to blow from the windows and a cool breeze began to whirl around the room. She sat back down and began to list the names of the other men involved with the Trollop.

The Masculine One immediately intervened. She shouted, "There was Mr. Ward, from New York, who couldn't get an erection because he was separated from his wife and still loved her. There was the one who looked like Michael Jackson, who gave her crabs." The Masculine One paused briefly, and then continued. "And I can't leave out Rollin with Roland. He tried to get to Mushy through the kids. You know, braiding my daughter's hair and making himself indispensable. After about a month, when he asked the Trollop to appear with him in court because he disobeyed the protection order placed on him by his ex-wife, the Trollop dumped him. And of course there was the Primate. The Primate was from Barbados and the Trollop thought that she would get a free trip to the island, but after a month, when no trip happened, she bailed and went back inside. Then Little Me put Mushy in charge, and I don't have to tell you what happened. After keeping the Primate for two years, I had to throw him out because he tried to beat Mushy up. Mushy actually accepted a ring from him, thinking that a man twenty-two years old and nine years her junior was being sincere. Finally, leaping, not jumping from the goddamn frying pan right into the fucking fire, and a mere two weeks after dumping the Primate, the Trollop got involved with Milton, got pregnant, and got married, in that order! That's what really happened! All that other shit is just what it is, bullshit!"

Dr. Townes continued to write. He asked, "Little Me, what are your thoughts about doing the drugs with Milton?"

Little Me stared at me, looking more and more reluctant to continue and still sweating profusely. "Everybody but Mushy was against doing the drugs, even the Trollop, and even Sick and Tired, although by the time things were really bad, Sick and Tired was the one in front most of the time and responsible for using. Mushy thought that doing the drugs with Milton would keep them together, but that was nonsense. I honestly didn't think I could handle the situation alone, which is why I kept out of it. You know, the drug stuff." Little Me started biting her nails. "I'll never forget the time I overheard Milton laughing and boasting with Brother Earl about the women they'd turned into monsters. He was proud of what he thought he'd turned me into. That stuck in my mind, and incensed the Masculine One, who always tried to fight him back when he hit any of the others or me. Nobody, not my family, not my friends, nobody knew I was involved with drugs. Only the small circle of people I knew from Milton or met through him knew I was doing drugs, and even they never knew how bad it was. I think I kept it a secret because the Perfectionist and the Gatekeeper took great care of the kids. While they did that, the Masculine One and the Perfectionist took care of getting me washed, dressed, and off to work every day, so I could keep a good paycheck coming in. The Gatekeeper kept the pretty face and attitude I needed to show my family and friends that things were just wonderful, even though they could not have been worse. I guess Sick and Tired and Mushy were what you might call functioning addicts. But after Sick and Tired and Mushy began freebasing with people other than Milton, I knew I had to get stronger, had to gain some kind of hold on myself somehow and quit doing drugs, because I knew they were getting progressively worse and I was most probably dangerously addicted at that point."

Dr. Townes repeated part of what Little Me said. "'I knew I had to get stronger somehow…' Do you realize in that instant, you were relying on yourself, Little Me? The operative word here is 'I.' You knew you were addicted to cocaine and crack during that time, and you knew you needed to get 'stronger, somehow,' didn't you? Did you seek professional help at that time to recover from your addiction?"

"No. We just banded together and helped them to stop. I did a lot of praying. I prayed to God and made a deal with Him that if I didn't get myself involved with losers anymore and that if I would take care of myself from that day forward, maybe, just maybe He would hear me and help them to get better, you know, not for me, but for my kids, and maybe for the others. God knows that I prayed that prayer and made deals with Him a whole lot of times before, and they still got me into trouble. I am sure the Lord got tired of hearing the same old tired prayer and decided to help me for the sake of my children." Little Me wasn't getting any relief from the cooling breeze. The sweat was beginning to pour from her face, and she was visibly uncomfortable.

"The next biggest problem was convincing Mushy that Milton wasn't redeemable, and that he would eventually kill her, which I realized meant killing everybody. That's where the others banded together with me. I didn't want Mushy or Sick and Tired out in front, if I could help it; only if I was genuinely sad about something that wasn't serious, and only temporarily then. Once we all agreed about Milton, the next step was getting Milton out of the house for good. I prayed he would leave quietly and leave me the way he found me, with a face my mother and kids could identify. That was important, since I discovered after we got married that he had a reputation for severely beating women straight into the hospital when he thought the relationship was over. 'I was ready to pull up anyway' were Milton's last words to me. My prayer was answered and he left on his own when I asked. I'll never forget that Sunday, November 19, 1989. I made a holiday out of it. It was my emancipation day; the day he left and the day I quit smoking crack." Little Me caught herself. "Did I say me, I meant Mushy and Sick and Tired quit, thanks to me, uh, I mean us." Little Me was clearly confused and her blouse was soaked from sweat that continued to drench her body.

"I was determined that I was going to turn my life around, so help me God. That's what it was, my life, not theirs, right? It's my life, not theirs. My life! Do you all hear that? It's my life! You are me and I am you! That's right, isn't it?" Little Me became frantic, glaring wildly at us.

Dr. Townes responded, "I'm amazed that you could identify your addiction, the severity of it, and then completely stop, all without professional help."

The Masculine One retorted, "Well, she didn't say they stopped doing drugs completely, just the crack."

Dr. Townes continued to ignore the Masculine One and asked Little Me to continue, but The Chatterbox seized the opportunity to blurt. "By the time that she ended things with Milton, the Trollop and Sick and Tired were already well on their way to becoming raving alcoholics. They have the booze bone, you know. They drank a lot of liquor, mostly Grandad 86 or 100. Straight with ice, too, no chaser, and they still snorted cocaine from time to time. We weren't married anymore, so the Trollop came out quite often. I stayed in the background, but I do admit that I enjoyed the drinking with them. The Trollop wasn't afraid to frequent bars by herself and did most of the time."

Little Me continued to glare at us; her eyes widening, and her eyeballs beading.

Dr. Townes mentioned the time; something he rarely did during a session. "I don't have any additional appointments today, and I'm very interested in having you continue if you don't mind, Little Me. You have been forthcoming, and I believe that the strides you are making are tremendous. I don't want to end the session here. If it's all right with you, I'd like to extend a courtesy by having you continue for as long as you wish this afternoon, at no additional expense to you. You're making so much progress, and I am very proud of you."

Little Me was drenched in sweat and shaking a bit. She asked for stronger and stronger breezes and then for air conditioning in the room but nothing seemed to comfort her. I was concerned about Little Me, since she didn't respond to the therapist's request. I acknowledged it for her and hoped he could hear me. He asked to be excused and was away for a short time. When he returned, he said that his reason for stepping out was because he needed more paper for his clipboard. He asked Little Me to continue, but she was too distressed to hear him.

"Of course, there is more, so much more, but we don't have enough time in this day to hear it all. I don't want to be in front, and I don't want to be in the Safe Room anymore today," Little Me said. I turned my head slightly, and then looked at Little Me. In an instant, she reverted back into the little girl, looking as frightened as she did when Mr. Peace was raping her.

Unaware of what was happening to Little Me, Dr. Townes continued his questioning. "I'm intrigued by your interpretation of the drug use. You seem to believe you weren't affected by the drugs yourself but were concerned about the others, especially Sick and Tired and Mushy. You said that because they were addicted, you needed to stop them, for their sake. Can you explain?"

Little Me continued to glare at us, as though she didn't know who we were, or for that matter where we were. She was visibly frightened. "They kept me from doing it all, even though I did it all. I can't understand how I could have done it all and wasn't the one doing it all. It's because I wasn't the one doing the drugs, it was them ... I mean, they, I mean, me, uh, you know, the drugs, they didn't affect me at all, or at least I don't think so, because if they had, why am I where I am now? I don't understand." Little Me paced back and forth around the Safe Room, faster and faster between the fireplace and the two large bow windows. Her appearance shifted as quickly as her pacing, back and forth, from older to younger, and then back again.

"I was in control, but I wasn't. Somebody had to have the presence of mind to pull out of it, right? I got strong. I was strong. I mean, they couldn't have been that far gone, could they? I enlisted the others and they joined me to get better. I did it. They helped. I think. It's because the crack was the worst of it. That would have killed us, really killed us, and my kids needed me to live. I needed to get better for my kids. Suffice it to say, liquor and drugs came in and out of my life, but never the crack again. Never that. I pulled in the reins on that one. It was just too dangerous and we all knew it. But, I don't want to think about this anymore. I don't want to be here anymore. I'm confused now. I can't think anymore. I'm not ever coming back here. NEVER!"

I looked at Little Me and watched as her eyes drifted upward, into their lids, and then she closed her eyes and fell to the floor. The others sat completely bewildered, with none apparently able or willing to assist.

Dr. Townes immediately requested the four angels, who suddenly appeared in each corner of the room. Jesus appeared and took Little Me into Him immediately. The others followed Little Me, and then Jesus disappeared into me.

When I returned to Dr. Townes' office, I was completely wet from perspiration. The large wet spot I left on the therapist's couch embarrassed me. I couldn't feel Little Me anywhere inside anymore. Little Me retreated once again to the deepest place inside and forced me to the front, which caused my skull to ache almost unbearably. I felt nauseous. "Doctor, I'm feeling extremely queasy right now," I moaned.

Dr. Townes replied, "I think we should let Little Me rest for a while. This may have been a little too much for her today. We'll meet again next week, and we'll meet in the Safe Room."

Too Much? For Her? I thought. I felt very insulted. It may have been too much for her, but it was equally too much for the others and too much for me. I was the one feeling pain. The pain radiated through my skull, not just hers, and I was feeling every swollen blood vessel, every pain. The ache this time was tremendous, and all the remedies in the world wouldn't have been enough. With each time she pushed further away, the hurt got worse.

For a moment, I had to forget about Little Me and her vanishing acts. We had to get home somehow. Fearing that I would be forced to drive, headache and all, I put the key in the ignition and started the motor, startling two deer that had wandered onto the property. I put the car into reverse, turned out of the parking space, and stopped short of the exit. I was starting to get nervous and my head was in excruciating pain. I begged the Masculine One to drive home, but true to form, she didn't want to cooperate, claiming that she was feeling the same pain. I put the car into drive and despite the lack of support, managed to get us all the way home.

Chapter Twenty-Three

I didn't go to my next scheduled appointment with the therapist. Then, days turned into weeks of missed appointments, and weeks turned into months of more missed appointments. Calls from Dr. Townes remained unanswered. I stopped going to therapy because Little Me had retreated. I couldn't tell if Little Me was just being impertinent, or if her retreat was for good. Although my head swirled with activity most of the time, there was no Little Me anywhere. She had pushed all the way into the deepest place this time. I didn't know how we were going to continue without her. She seemed to be gone; an impossibility to be sure, unless of course we were dead and didn't know it. At the same time, both the Perfectionist and Masculine One left me in a most untenable position with their constant arguments over who would be better suited to run our life. It was evident to me that should we ever go back into therapy, we would have to start from scratch. The Masculine One always maintained that the therapist was some sort of evil Svengali who concocted the entire thing to make us crazy just so he could cure us and make money on a book about us later. They both maintained that until we began this therapy, Little Me remained tucked away, safely and neatly, and that we were fine. However, we weren't fine, and it was foolish to think otherwise.

"We could simply overrule her and take over completely, couldn't we?" the Masculine One asked the Perfectionist. "I believe the two of us are our best option. If she wants to stay down, keep her down! Keep her down. We can handle things ourselves!" The thought of the Masculine One and the Perfectionist in front concurrently, in complete control of us, was simply absurd. Our life would be filled with rage, anger, eating disorders, and a feigned perception of arrogant perfection. I reminded them that we really didn't have the right to make decisions like the one they were proposing.

I jumped into the argument. "We need to go back into therapy to figure this out," I shouted. Sick and Tired was beset with dread. "You're starting it all over again, just like the first time, talking about therapy! I can't take this!" she shrieked.

"This is obvious nonsense!" I shouted. "Neither of you can handle us all the time."

All the others agreed with me for a change, overruling the Masculine One and the Perfectionist.

The Masculine One backed off. "Oh, quiet, you bitches!" she snapped. "Besides, I know we can't overrule Little Me! She's the damn boss." Although the Masculine One was not thrilled with the fact that Little Me was boss, she was completely accurate in her assessment of our position relative to hers. There was no overruling Little Me. That was impossible. In the past, whenever we took over, each time was because Little Me wanted it that way. Our participation in life, what we knew or didn't know along the way was always because Little Me wanted it that way. We were always participants, however reluctantly, and participated at the will of Little Me. She was the one ultimately responsible for herself and our fate, and only she could decide if we would have a fate at all.

"What's the point of going back to the therapist?" asked the Masculine One. "I don't think we need him anymore. He was only really interested in Little Me anyway, right? Well, guess what? She's not coming out, so again I ask, what's the point?"

I screamed loudly into the air, startling Victor, who was watching television in bed on the other side of the room. There was yet another storm brewing inside my head, and I was hard pressed to stop it. The Masculine One was pushing her way past the others to the uppermost part, just above the surface where I was. I found myself playing both politician and traffic cop, excusing the Masculine One's apparent rudeness to the others as she stepped wildly to reach where I was.

When the Masculine One pushed past the Perfectionist, the Perfectionist blurted, "One of us obviously wants to separate from the whole! We need cohesiveness."

Incensed, the Masculine One yelled, "What the hell crap is that? Just say fuckin' togetherness already! You make me sick!" Her voice resonated from outside my mouth in front of my husband, frightening him out of a light sleep.

"Huh, were you talking to me?" he asked timidly, half asleep. I explained that there was turmoil in my head again, and that it had nothing to do with him. He shrugged his broad shoulders, shook his head, frowned slightly, and then gave me a reassuring smile.

I couldn't stand myself anymore. I longed so much for peace of mind. I would have accepted anybody else's mind but my own and these others. I couldn't stand owning the same existence as these other people Little Me created. We needed to go back into therapy. I never should have stopped it. The meds were quickly running out, and I could feel Sick and Tired strengthening and growing more bold. I walked over to the bed, reached in, and kissed my husband's forehead. "Don't mind me, honey, I am just thrashing out some things in my mind, and sometimes it gets pretty loud."

The Masculine One was extremely agitated. I implored her to keep the yelling to the inside of our head and not to use our outer voice for fear that it would spook our husband. *He can only take so much of this*, I thought. Big Fat, Mushy, and the Trollop were frightened by the Masculine One and retreated even deeper than where the Masculine One had originally pushed them, almost to where they could no longer be felt.

Then she shouted loudly, "Frankly, I'm weary of Little Me. Furthermore, don't think I don't know you all wish I would just go away like she did, that you don't need me. But you do. I'll be damned if I will apologize for being tough. I am tough because I needed to be, for us! Yeah, I'm tough, and I am glad I'm tough, because you bitches aren't. If it wasn't for me, we would have died a long, long time ago, and Little Me knows that all too well! That's why I'm here. But make no mistake bitches; I can leave the body. I CAN do that, you know. I don't have to wait for some money grubbing hypnotherapist to push me out. I have a good mind to leave this fucking bird's nest anyway! How did Milton say it, 'I was gonna pull up anyway?' In fact, we all can leave if we want to. We don't have to come out just because she tells us to. She's not the only one growing around here. We are ageless, just like she said she was. We don't have to hang around if we don't want to, and she can be left alone to make her own damn way from now on." The Masculine One was more furious than she usually was, and I suspect that it was because, in reality, she was the most fearful of being pushed out if Little Me was healed.

"You're an emotional train wreck!" the Perfectionist shouted at the Masculine One. The others remained silent. Whenever there was an argument between the Masculine One and the Perfectionist, everyone was too afraid to take sides, but I needed to stand my ground. What the Masculine One was saying was patently absurd. Didn't she even realize what she was saying? If we all left Little Me while she was so far inside, life as we knew it would be over. Besides, where would we go? And what would happen to our body?

"The nut house is filled with people exactly like what you are proposing for us to do!" I shouted. "If we leave, especially while Little Me is in retreat, the body would be nothing more than a shell. Is that what you want? Do you want the body to end up in some asylum, in a rocking chair, staring aimlessly at a blank wall and sucking cream of wheat from a straw?"

The Perfectionist declared, "What we need is to find the strongest, emotionally, to stay in the front. That way, Little Me can stay just where she is now, protected but totally aware of our goings on, like before. That's what we need to do, and of course the best in this case would be me, because I am the closest thing we have to perfection, and you all know it!"

Just when I thought that there was some semblance of consensus, some inkling of rational thinking, the Perfectionist unnerved me. The others were unnerved as well, and remained eerily silent. It became apparent that the

Perfectionist indeed wanted to dominate the rest of us and take over completely for Little Me. Of course splitting was a thought that I had only considered briefly, then threw out as a ridiculous notion borne by the revelation of having been named the Gatekeeper during therapy. But she was serious, and if Little Me stayed away, it could derail all of the progress that we all made since the beginning of therapy. If no one else would speak up, at least I knew that she was the wrong person to be front and center. The best and the strongest would certainly hold all of us together all right. The problem was, Little Me needed to be that person, not us, and certainly not the Perfectionist. I needed to get us to the therapist quickly. Perhaps I could quietly lobby some of the others to go back to therapy and overrule anyone who didn't want to.

Chapter Twenty-Four

A year had gone by and I still hadn't gone back to therapy. The only way I even knew that the year had passed was because someone said as much. *A year already*— I remembered thinking. The meds had run out and on occasion, my brain swirled with that water-on-the-brain feeling that happens when stopping medication abruptly. Little Me had disappeared, it seemed, although I knew she had to be somewhere, or I'd be dead. There was no way that I could simply cease to exist, and catatonia was also out of the question, so I did my job. I got up every day, at the same time each morning, got ready for work, and survived as best I could. That was, after all, what the therapist told Little Me that she was: a survivor.

Perhaps I could be one too, I thought.

When I got to work, I noticed I had a beautiful bouquet of flowers in a vase that usually sat on Marissa's desk. They were the kind I loved, a mixture of lilacs, gardenias, and lots of lavender. The fragrant aroma of the flowers was as welcome as the thought that perhaps Marissa was still my friend. Peeking from behind the door to my office, Marissa asked if she could come in. She stood by the door and smiled shyly. "I just didn't know how to react. How do you react to something like that?" she asked. "I just needed some time to understand."

She didn't have to say a word, but I knew she needed to. I just hugged her. That was it. She wanted to know if I was going to go back to therapy. I didn't know the answer to that question and certainly didn't want to aggravate the others with the likelihood of it. She was still going, and of course Dr. Townes asked her how I was doing. I said I hoped they didn't talk about me, and she said there was no way she would. I knew she was lying; everybody was worried about me.

I rustled through my pocketbook, found Dr. Townes' card, and called him. I suspected that perhaps it could have been Little Me, or anyone else who gave me the nudge. None of that mattered. What did matter was that if I did go back, I would be going back with a completely new perspective. At least this time I would go in knowing who I was. I called the therapist and made an appointment, much to the disappointment of the Masculine One, who was overruled, again.

On the day of my appointment, the Perfectionist dressed me in a beautiful black, blue, and white print dress. Big Fat prepared a lavish meal of French toast, eggs, turkey bacon, and tea. I was oddly secure about my decision, despite the mêlée that started in my head.

Dr. Townes was happy to see me, and on a level that I still can't explain, I was glad I came. He walked with me into his office, and I immediately noticed that he had redecorated. I chuckled when I noticed that his brand new desk was cluttered with papers and debris, just like his old one was before. *Some things just never change,* I thought.

I concentrated on the clock on the wall as the therapist directed, and before I knew it, I could see the old Victorian house in the distance. I rushed toward it, tripping a couple of times on the lawn's thick green grass, and stopped briefly to pick the fresh lavender. I opened the large red door and noticed that the table in the center of the foyer was gone. In its place was a beautiful grandfather clock where the French doors used to be. Now there were two sets of French doors, on either side of the wall where the lovely grandfather clock stood. I was just in time to hear the clock sound the Westminster chime, loudly, like the bells that ring in a church, and like the clock on my living room wall. I walked through the French doors on the right and into the room where Little Me had placed the pretty green and white flowered and striped curtains on the large bow windows on my first day.

Dr. Townes asked, "Where are you?"

I responded excitedly, "I am in the Safe Room."

"What are you wearing?" he asked.

"The same dress I wore to the office today, and I am me, the Gatekeeper."

One by one, each entered the room as they had so many times before. The Perfectionist waltzed in and sat on the comfy couch near the fireplace. With a flash of light and smoke, all of which seemed a bit overdone by now, the Masculine One arrived like a leftover lightning bolt after the threat of a storm that never happened. She sat in a smart looking leather chair that appeared in front of the couch. Finally, the Trollop, Mushy, Sick and Tired, and Big Fat strolled in and sat.

"I would like to speak to Little Me," Dr. Townes said.

"She's not here, Doctor," I said.

Dr. Townes asked for Little Me, but I didn't know if she would come into the room. He continued to coax Little Me, and then eventually a little voice in my ear asked me to look out of the large bow window at the tree to the left of the center. It was Little Me. She was waiving her tiny hand and leaning against the tree. I implored her to join us in the room. When I looked back outside at the tree, Little Me was skipping and twirling around it. She twirled her way to the front of the house, smelling the flowers as she skipped. She flung open the French doors that were to the left of the Grandfather clock in the foyer and ran into my arms.

"I'm here," she said to Dr. Townes.

"How are you dressed today?" he asked.

"I have on my pretty dress with a white pinafore on it, and my hair is in ponytails. I have on white socks with ruffles and black patent Mary Janes." Little Me walked over to the Perfectionist and sat down next to her. The Masculine One rose from where she was sitting and sat on the left side of Little Me as the Perfectionist sat on the right, so that Little Me was between them, protected, on the comfy couch. "I'm not ready to come outside of the Safe Room, and that's just gonna have to be okay for now."

We all sighed, long and purposeful, and then the group settled in for whatever the therapist had planned for the day's session. As I looked around the room at everyone there, it appeared that I was indeed back to the beginning of the block, getting ready to go around it once again, just to get to the corner. This time it was different, though. I was anxious but not afraid. I took a seat in a large pink cushy chair that I had just brought into the room and continued to watch. Little Me was sitting on Big Fat's voluminous lap, disappearing between the folds of her massive arms while Dr. Townes tried to keep her attention during the session. Sick and Tired was lying in a fetal position on the far end of a large couch, beside Mushy and the Trollop. The Chatterbox continued to interrupt the others, weighing in on whatever she thought they left out.

I positioned my chair at the large bow window, and looked out at the beautiful garden, wondering if we would ever really get well, and what it would take to get there. Would we really have to converge until there was only a trace of our individual consciousness left inside Little Me, or would we retain some semblance of our own individuality? Would Little Me ever emerge outside the Safe Room and take charge of her life for good? And if she did, what did that mean for us?

After a time, the four angels appeared in their places, and I called out to Dr. Townes. "The angels are here. Is it time to leave?"

He responded, "Yes, I am afraid so. Jesus is standing there, waiting for you all to enter into Him."

As He stood by the fireplace, the group entered Jesus as they always did. Little Me jumped into Jesus' arms and hugged Him. Then she entered. When Jesus walked over to me, He stood completely still. Without uttering a sound, He smiled at me, with His arms outstretched and I could feel his words. "Each time I enter into you, know that I am always with you, Gatekeeper, and I will give you peace." I stood there, motionless for a time. Jesus entered me, and soon, I was back in Dr. Townes' office, thanking him for the session, and making another appointment for the next week.

On the drive home, I thought about the peace that Jesus said He would give me, and it made me smile. *One day I might just understand what He meant*, I thought.

Then gradually, in little spurts and then in bursts, I began to feel some nice feelings, somewhat better than ease and almost peaceful, as the Masculine One drove us home.

I felt for the first time that I understood something about my life. *Peace is such a relative term. It's full of levels*, I thought. *For now, this level is good.* I watched the sun and felt its warmth against my face. I admired the beauty of the blue sky and the wildflowers growing along the side of the long winding road away from the therapist's office. The others chattered softly in my head; they knew that therapy was a necessary evil, and we would just have to manage the way we had before, with me in front and the others helping out where necessary from time to time. We were going to be best friends, whether we liked it or not.

After finding a good parking space and satisfying the Perfectionist's penchant for avoiding dings, I walked inside the house and up to the bedroom, where Victor was lying down, watching TV.

I leaned in for a quick peck on the cheek and Sick and Tired whispered, "This journey won't be no crystal stair, you know."

I smiled to myself, realizing that all this time, Sick and Tired had the right metaphor for our life without even knowing it. Life wasn't a crystal stair for us—never was, just as she always reminded me. But that's a good thing. Fine crystal is fragile and must be handled carefully, or it will shatter into a thousand pieces. Because crystal is glass, it's transparent. We aren't transparent, because we have substance. We aren't fragile either, and although we are still together apart, we aren't shattered. Life for us may not be a crystal stair, but the best part of that is, we won't ever break.

To be continued? Perhaps, as long as life does the same.

NOTES

4019255

Made in the USA